D0773289

MAIGRET'S MEMOIRS

Translated from the French by

Jean Stewart

MAIGRET'S MEMOIRS

GEORGES SIMENON

A Helen and Kurt Wolff Book

Harcourt Brace Jovanovich, Publishers

San Diego   New York   London

Requests for permission to make copies of any
part of the work should be mailed to: Permissions,
Harcourt Brace Jovanovich, Publishers, Orlando,
Florida 32887.

Library of Congress Cataloging in Publication Data

Simenon, Georges, 1903-
    Maigret's memoirs.

    Translation of: Mémoires de Maigret.
    "A Helen and Kurt Wolff book."
    I. Title.
PQ2637.I53M4513   1985   843'.912   85-8591
ISBN 0-15-155148-0

Designed by Matthew Simpson
Printed in the United States of America

First American edition

A   B   C   D   E

MAIGRET'S
MEMOIRS

1

*Which affords me a welcome opportunity of
explaining my relations with Monsieur Simenon*

It was in 1927 or 1928. I have no memory for dates and
I am not one of those who keep a careful record of their
doings, a habit that is not uncommon in our profession
and that has proved of considerable use and even profit
to some people. And it was only quite recently that I
remembered the notebooks in which my wife, for a long
time without my knowledge and indeed behind my back,
had stuck any newspaper stories that referred to me.

Because of a certain case that gave us some trouble that
year—I could probably discover the exact date, but I
don't have the courage to go and look through those
notebooks.

It doesn't matter. At any rate, I remember quite clearly
what the weather was like. It was a nondescript day at
the beginning of winter, one of those colorless gray-and-
white days that I am tempted to call "administrative
days," because one has the impression that nothing interesting can happen in so dull an atmosphere, while in the

office, out of sheer boredom, one feels an urge to bring one's files up to date, to deal with reports that have been lying around a long time, to tackle current business ferociously but without heart.

If I stress the unrelieved grayness of the day it is not from any desire to be picturesque, but in order to show how commonplace the incident itself was, swamped in the trivial happenings of a commonplace day.

It was about ten o'clock in the morning. We had finished making our reports about half an hour earlier; the conference had been short.

Nowadays even the least well-informed members of the public know more or less what's involved in the conferences at the Police Judiciaire, but in those days most Parisians would have found it hard to say even which government service was housed on Quai des Orfèvres.

At nine o'clock sharp a bell summons the various heads of sections to the Chief's big office, whose windows overlook the Seine. There is no glamour about these gatherings. You go there smoking your pipe or your cigarette, usually with a file tucked under your arm. The day hasn't got started yet, and, for most people, still vaguely smells of café au lait and croissants. You shake hands. You gossip, leisurely, waiting for everybody to show up.

Then each in turn informs the Chief about what has been happening in his sector. A few remain standing, sometimes looking out the window to watch the buses and taxis crossing Pont Saint-Michel.

Contrary to general belief, we do not talk exclusively about crime.

"How's your daughter, Priollet? Her measles?"

I remember hearing recipes knowledgeably detailed.

More serious problems are also discussed, of course;

for instance, that of some deputy's or minister's son who has been behaving foolishly, who willfully persists in his folly, and whom it is imperative to bring back to his senses without causing a scandal. Or that of a rich foreigner who has recently taken up residence in some grand hotel on the Champs-Elysées, and about whom the government has begun to worry. Or that of a little girl picked up in the street a few days previously, whom no relative has claimed, although her picture has appeared in all the newspapers.

This is a gathering of professional people, and events are considered from a strictly professional point of view, without useless talk, so that everything becomes very simple. It's all in the day's work, so to speak.

"Well now, Maigret, haven't you arrested your Pole on Rue de Birague yet?"

Let me hasten to say that I have nothing against Poles as such. If I happen to speak of them fairly often, it's not because I consider them a particularly aggressive or delinquent people. The fact is merely that at that time France, being short of labor, imported Poles by the thousands and settled them in the mines in the North. They were collected haphazardly in their own country, whole villages at a time, men, women, and children, and piled into trains, just as, at an earlier time, black labor was recruited.

The majority of them have proved to be first-class workers, and many have become respected citizens. Nevertheless, there was a certain proportion of riffraff, as was only to be expected, and for some time this riffraff gave us a good deal of trouble.

I am trying to convey the atmosphere to the reader by talking this way, somewhat disconnectedly, about the things that were preoccupying me at that time.

"I would like to keep him on the run for two or three days longer, Chief. So far he's led us nowhere. He's sure to end up by meeting some accomplices."

"The Minister's getting impatient because of the press. . . ."

Always the press! And always, among the powers that be, that dread of the press, of public opinion. No sooner has a crime been committed than we are urged to find a culprit immediately, at all costs.

We are practically told, after a few days: "Put somebody or other in jail in the meantime, just to satisfy public opinion."

I will probably revert to this point. In any case, it was not the Pole that we were discussing that morning, but a burglary that had recently been committed by means of a new technique, which is an uncommon thing.

Three days earlier, on Boulevard Saint-Denis, in the middle of the day, just as most of the shops had closed for lunch, a truck had stopped in front of a small jewelry store. Some men had unloaded an enormous packing case, which they had put down close to the door, and had gone off again with the truck.

Hundreds of people had passed in front of that case without thinking twice about it. As for the jeweler, when he came back from the restaurant where he had had lunch, he knit puzzled brows.

And when he had shifted the case, which had now become very light, he discovered that a hole had been cut in the side that touched the door, and another hole in the door itself, and that, of course, all his shelves had been ransacked, and his safe as well.

This was the sort of unsensational inquiry that is liable to take months and requires the largest number of men.

The burglars had not left a single fingerprint, nor any compromising object.

The fact that the method was a new one made it impossible for us to hunt in any known category of thieves.

We had nothing but the packing case, an ordinary box although a very large one, and for the past three days a round dozen inspectors had been visiting all manufacturers of packing cases, and all firms making use of the largest size.

I had just returned to my office, where I had begun to write a report, when the internal telephone rang.

"Is that you, Maigret? Will you come to my room for a moment?"

Nothing surprising about that either. Every day, or almost every day, the Big Chief used to call me at least once to his office, apart from the conference. I had known him since my childhood; he had often spent his vacations close to our home in Allier, and he had been a friend of my father's.

And this particular chief was, in my eyes, the real chief in the fullest sense of the word, the chief under whom I had served my first term at the Police Judiciaire, who, without actually protecting me, had kept a discreet eye on me from above, and whom I had watched, in his black coat and bowler hat, walking alone under fire toward the door of the house in which Bonnot and his gang had for two days been resisting police and gendarmes, or armed police.

I am referring to Xavier Guichard, with his mischievous eyes and his white hair, as long as a poet's.

"Come in, Maigret."

The daylight was so dull that morning that the green-shaded lamp on his desk was turned on. Close by, in an armchair, I saw a young man, who rose to offer me his hand when we were introduced to one another.

"Chief Inspector Maigret. Monsieur Georges Sim, who's a journalist. . . ."

"Not a journalist, a novelist," the young man protested, smilingly.

Xavier Guichard smiled, too. And he had a whole range of smiles, which could express all the various shades of what he was thinking. He also had at his disposal a sort of irony, perceptible only to those who knew him well and which, to others, sometimes made him appear a simpleton.

He spoke to me with the utmost seriousness, as if we were concerned with an important matter, a prominent personality.

"For his novel-writing, Monsieur Sim needs to know how the Police Judiciaire functions. As he has just explained to me, a good many dramatic stories wind up in this building. He has also made it clear that it's not so much the workings of the police machine that he wants to study in detail—since he has been able to get information about these elsewhere—but, rather, the atmosphere in which these operations take place."

I merely glanced at the young man, who must have been about twenty-four and who was thin, with hair almost as long as the Chief's, and of whom the least I can say is that he seemed to have no lack of confidence about anything, least of all about himself.

"Will you show him around, Maigret?"

And just as I was moving toward the door I heard the fellow Sim remark:

"Excuse me, Monsieur Guichard, but you've forgotten to mention to the Chief Inspector . . ."

"Oh, yes, you're quite right. Monsieur Sim, as he has reminded us, is not a journalist. So there's no danger of his reporting to the newspapers things that ought to remain unpublished. He has promised me, without being asked, to use in his novels only whatever he may see or hear among us, and that in a form sufficiently altered to create no difficulties for us."

I can still hear the Chief adding gravely, as he bent forward to look at his mail:

"You needn't worry, Maigret. He has given me his word."

All the same, I felt already—and my feeling was subsequently confirmed—that Xavier Guichard had let himself be led astray. Not only by the youthful audacity of his visitor, but also on account of something I only discovered later. The Chief, apart from his profession, had one passion: archaeology. He belonged to several learned societies and had written a fat book (which I have never read) about the remote origins of Paris and its surroundings.

Young Sim had discovered this, whether or not by chance, and had made a point of talking to him about it.

Was it for this reason that I had been sent for personally? Almost every day somebody at the Quais gets the job of showing visitors around. Generally these are distinguished foreigners, or those connected in some way with the police of their country, or sometimes merely influential voters, come up from the provinces and proudly exhibiting a card from their deputy. It has become a routine. There is a little lecture that everybody has more or less learned by heart, like guides to historical monuments.

But usually a regular inspector serves the purpose, and the visitor has to be somebody very important for the head of a section to be disturbed.

"If you like," I proposed, "we'll go first to the anthropometric section."

"If it isn't too much bother, I'd rather begin with the waiting room."

This was my first surprise. He said it quite nicely, too, with a disarming glance, explaining:

"You understand; I would like to follow the route that your clients usually follow."

"In that case, you ought to start at a police station, since most of them spend the night there before being brought to us."

He replied, calmly:

"I visited a police station last night."

He took no notes. He had neither notebook nor fountain pen. He stayed for several minutes in the tall-windowed waiting room, where, in black frames, the photographs of members of the police killed on duty are displayed.

"How many casualties each year, on an average?"

Then he asked to see my office. Now it so happened that at that time workmen were busy redoing it. I was provisionally installed on the mezzanine, in an office in the oldest governmental style, thick with dust, with black wooden furniture and a coal-burning stove of the kind you still see in certain provincial railroad stations.

This was the office in which I had started my professional life, in which I had worked as inspector for some fifteen years, and I must admit that I harbored a certain fondness for that huge stove, whose iron bars I loved to see glowing red in winter, and which I used to stoke up to the brim. This was not so much an inveterate habit as a trick to keep my composure. In the middle of a difficult interrogation I would get up and poke the fire at length, then throw in noisy shovelfuls of coal, looking quite bland, while my client stared at me in bewilderment.

And the fact is that when at last I had a modern office at my disposal, equipped with central heating, I missed my old stove, but I would never have been allowed, nor did I ever make the request—which would not have been granted—to take it with me into my new premises.

I must apologize for lingering over these details, but I know more or less what I'm getting at.

My guest looked at my pipes, my ashtrays, the black marble clock on the mantelpiece, the little enamel basin behind the door, and the towel that always smells like a wet dog.

He asked me no technical questions. The files did not seem to interest him in the slightest.

"This stairway takes us to the laboratory."

There, too, he stared at the ceiling, which was partly glass, at the walls, at the floor, and at the dummy that is used for certain reconstructions, but he paid no attention either to the laboratory itself, with its complicated apparatus, or to the work going on there.

Out of habit, I tried to explain:

"By magnifying several hundred times any written text, and comparing it . . ."

"I know. I know."

And then he asked me, casually:

"Have you read Hans Gross?"

I had never heard the name mentioned. I have since learned that it was that of an Austrian examining magistrate who, in the 1880s, held the first chair of scientific criminology at the University of Vienna.

My visitor, however, had read Hans Gross's two fat volumes. He had read everything, quantities of books of whose very existence I was ignorant and whose titles he quoted at me in an offhand manner.

"Follow me along this passage, and I'll show you the Records Office, where we keep the files of . . ."

"I know. I know."

I was beginning to find him irritating. It looked as if he had put me to all this bother solely in order to stare at walls and ceilings and floors, to stare at us all, as if he were drawing up an inventory.

"We'll find a crowd in the anthropometric offices right now. They'll have finished with the women, and it'll be the men's turn. . . ."

There were some twenty of these, stark naked, who had been rounded up during the night and were waiting their turn to be measured and photographed.

"In short," the young man said to me, "all I've still got to see is the Special Infirmary."

I frowned.

"Visitors are not admitted."

It is one of the least-known places, where criminals and suspects are put through a number of mental tests by police doctors.

"Paul Bourget used to watch the proceedings," my visitor calmly replied. "I shall ask for permission."

The fact is that I retained a wholly uninteresting memory of him, as uninteresting as the weather itself that day. If I made no effort to cut short his visit, it was primarily because of the Chief's recommendation, and also because I had nothing important to do and it was, after all, a way of killing time.

He happened to pass through my office again later, sat down, and held out his tobacco pouch to me.

"I see you're a pipe smoker, too. I like pipe smokers."

There were, as usual, a good half-dozen pipes lying around, and he examined them with a connoisseur's eye.

"What case are you on at the moment?"

In my most professional tone I told him about the robbery where the packing case had been left at the door of the jewelry store, pointing out that this was the first time this technique had been used.

"No," he said to me. "It was used eight years ago in New York, at a shop on Eighth Avenue."

He must have been pleased with himself, but I admit that he did not seem to be boasting. He was smoking his pipe gravely, as if to add ten years to his age and put himself on an equal footing with the mature man that I already was.

"You see, Chief Inspector, I'm not interested in professionals. Their psychology offers no problems. They are just men doing their own job, and that's all."

"What *are* you interested in?"

"The others. Those who are made like you and me, and who end up one fine day by killing somebody without being prepared to."

"There are very few of those."

"I know."

"Apart from crimes of passion . . ."

"There's nothing interesting about them either."

That's all I remember of that encounter. I must have spoken to him incidentally of a case on which I had been busy a few months earlier, just because professionals were not involved in it, a case concerning a young girl and a pearl necklace.

"Thank you, Chief Inspector. I hope I shall have the pleasure of meeting you again."

Privately, I said to myself: "I sincerely hope not."

11

•   •   •

Weeks passed, then months. Once, in the middle of winter, I thought I recognized the fellow Sim in the main corridor of the Police Judiciaire, pacing up and down.

One morning I found on my desk, beside my mail, a little book with a revolting illustrated cover, such as are displayed by newspaper dealers and read by salesgirls. It was called: *The Girl with the Pearl Necklace*, and the name of the author was Georges Sim.

I didn't have the curiosity to read it. I read few books, and no popular novels. I don't even know where I put the book, a paperback, printed on cheap paper—probably in the wastepaper basket, and I thought no more about it for several days.

Then one morning I found an identical book in the same place on my desk, and, after that, each morning a new copy appeared beside my mail.

It was some time before I noticed that my inspectors, particularly Lucas, were glancing at me with amusement. At last Lucas said to me, after beating about the bush for a long time, as we made our way to the Brasserie Dauphine one day for a drink before lunch:

"So you're a character in a novel now, Chief."

He pulled the book out of his pocket.

"Have you read it?"

He confessed that it was Janvier, the youngest member of the squad at that time, who had been putting a copy of the book on my desk each morning.

"It's quite like you in some ways, you'll see."

He was right. It was like me to the extent that a sketch scribbled on the marble top of a café table by an amateur caricaturist is like a flesh-and-blood human being.

It made me bigger and clumsier than I really am, peculiarly ponderous, so to speak.

As for the story, it was unrecognizable, and I was made to use some quite unexpected methods, to say the least.

That same evening I found my wife with the book in her hands.

"The woman in the dairy gave it to me. Apparently it's about you. I haven't had time to read it yet."

What could I do? As the man Sim had promised, no newspaper was involved. The book was not a serious work, but a cheap publication, to which it would have been absurd to attach any importance.

He had used my real name. But he might have replied that there are quite a number of Maigrets in the world. I merely promised myself to receive him somewhat coldly if I happened to meet him again, convinced, meanwhile, that he would avoid setting foot in the Police Judiciaire.

In this I was mistaken. One day when I knocked at the Chief's door without having been sent for, to ask his advice on some point, he said:

"Come in, Maigret. I was just going to call you. Our friend Sim is here."

No signs of embarrassment about our friend Sim. On the contrary, complete self-confidence and a bigger pipe than ever in his mouth.

"How are you, Chief Inspector?"

And Guichard explained:

"He's just been reading me a few passages from something he's written about our place."

"I know about it."

Xavier Guichard's eyes were full of laughter, but this time it was of me that he seemed to be making fun.

"Then he told me some rather relevant things, which may interest you. He'll repeat them to you."

"It's quite simple. Until now, in France, in books, with

very few exceptions, the sympathetic character has always been the offender, whereas the police have been exposed to ridicule, if not worse."

Guichard was nodding approvingly.

"Quite true, isn't it?"

And it was, in fact, quite true. Not only in books, but also in daily life. I was reminded of a rather painful episode in my early days, when I was serving in the Public Roads Squad. I was on the point of arresting a pickpocket outside a Métro station when the fellow began yelling something—possibly "Stop, thief!"

Instantly a score of people fell on me. I explained to them that I was a policeman, that the man now making his escape was a habitual criminal. I am convinced that they all believed me. They nonetheless managed to delay me by every possible means, thus allowing my pickpocket to get away.

"Well," Guichard went on, "our friend Sim is proposing to write a series of novels in which the police will be shown in their true light."

I made a face, which the Chief did not fail to notice.

"More or less in their true light," he corrected himself. "You follow me? His book is only a rough draft of what he plans to do."

"He has made use of my name."

I thought the young man would be covered with confusion and would apologize. Not at all.

"I hope you weren't offended, Chief Inspector. I couldn't help it. When I have imagined a character under a particular name, I find it quite impossible to change it. I tried out all possible combinations of syllables to replace those of the name Maigret, but in vain. In the end, I gave up. It wouldn't have been *my* character any longer."

He said "*my* character," quite calmly, and the amazing

thing was that I never flinched, possibly because of Xavier Guichard and the mischievously twinkling eyes he kept fixed on me.

"He is thinking this time not of a popular series but of what he calls . . . What did you call it, Monsieur Sim?"

"Semiliterature."

"And you're counting on me to . . ."

"I would like to know you better."

I told you at the beginning: his self-assurance was complete. I really believe that was the secret of his strength. It was partly through this that he had already succeeded in winning over the Chief, who was interested in every type of human being and who announced to me, without a smile:

"He is only twenty-four."

"I find it hard to construct a character unless I know how he behaves at every moment of the day. For instance, I won't be able to talk about millionaires until I have seen one in his dressing gown eating his boiled egg for breakfast."

This happened a long time ago, and I wonder now for what mysterious reason we listened to all this without bursting out laughing.

"In short, you'd like . . ."

"To know you better, to watch you living and working."

Of course, the Chief gave me no orders. I would no doubt have rebelled. For quite some time, I felt uncertain whether he wasn't playing a practical joke on me, since he had retained a certain Latin Quarter streak in his character, from the days when the Latin Quarter still went in for hoaxes.

It was probably in order not to seem to be taking the whole affair too seriously that I said, shrugging my shoulders:

"Whenever you like."

Then young Sim jumped up delightedly.

"Right away."

Once more, in retrospect, it may seem ridiculous. The dollar was worth I don't know what fantastic sums. Americans used to light their cigars with thousand-franc notes. Montmartre was teeming with black musicians, and rich, middle-aged ladies let themselves be robbed of their jewelry by Argentine gigolos at tea dances. The Vice Squad was overwhelmed by orgiastic parties in the Bois de Boulogne, which they scarcely dared interrupt for fear of disturbing diplomatic personalities having their fun.

Women had short hair and short skirts, and men wore pointed shoes and trousers tight around the ankles.

This explains nothing, I know. But everything is interconnected. And I can still see young Sim coming into my office next morning, as if he were one of my inspectors, remarking kindly: "Don't let me disturb you . . ." and going to sit in a corner.

He still took no notes. He asked few questions. He tended, rather, to make assertions. He explained to me subsequently—and it doesn't follow that I believed him— that a man's reactions to an assertion are more revealing than his replies to a specific question.

One day at noon, when we went for a drink at the Brasserie Dauphine, Lucas, Janvier, and I, as was our frequent cusom, he followed us.

And one morning, at the conference, I found him installed in a corner of the Chief's office.

This went on for several months. When I asked him if he was writing, he answered:

"Popular novels, still, to earn my living. From four to

eight in the morning. By eight o'clock I've finished my day's work. I will only start on semiliterary novels when I feel ready for it."

I don't know what he meant by that, but, after I had invited him to lunch one Sunday on Boulevard Richard-Lenoir and had introduced him to my wife, he suddenly stopped coming to the Quai des Orfèvres.

It seemed odd not to see him in his corner, getting up when I got up, following me when I went out, and accompanying me step by step through the offices.

During that spring I received an invitation that was, to say the least, unexpected.

Georges Sim has the honor of inviting you to the christening of his boat, the Ostrogoth, *which will be performed by the Curé of Notre-Dame on Tuesday next, at the Square du Vert-Galant.*

I did not go. I learned from the police of that district that for three days and three nights a rowdy gang kept up a tremendous uproar on board a boat moored right in the middle of Paris and flying all its flags.

Once, as I crossed the Pont-Neuf, I saw this boat and, at the foot of the mast, somebody sitting at a typewriter, wearing a master mariner's cap.

The following week the boat was gone, and the Square du Vert-Galant had resumed its usual appearance.

More than a year later, I received another invitation, written this time on one of our fingerprint cards.

Georges Simenon has the honor of inviting you to the Anthropometrical Ball, which will be held at the Boule Blanche to celebrate the launching of his detective stories.

17

Sim had turned into Simenon.

More precisely, feeling himself now fully adult, perhaps, he had resumed his real name.

I did not bother with it. I did not go to the ball, but I learned next day that the Chief Police Commissioner had been present.

Through the newspapers. The same newspapers that informed me, on the front page, that Chief Inspector Maigret had just made his sensational entry into detective fiction.

That morning, when I arrived at the Quais and climbed the great staircase, I was met with sly smiles and amused averted faces.

My inspectors did their utmost to keep straight faces. My colleagues, at the conference, pretended to treat me with unwonted respect.

Only the Big Chief behaved as if nothing had happened and asked me, with an absent-minded air:

"And what about you, Maigret? How are things going?"

In the shops of the Richard-Lenoir district, there was not a shopkeeper who failed to show my wife the paper with my name in large letters, and, impressed, ask her:

"It *is* your husband, isn't it?"

It was I, alas!

2

*In which it is argued that the naked truth is
often unconvincing and that dressed-up truths
may seem more real than life*

When the news got around that I was writing this book,
and then that Simenon's publisher, without having read
it, before I had even finished the first chapter, had offered
to publish it, I was conscious of the somewhat dubious
approval of my friends. They were saying, I'm convinced:
"So Maigret's taking his turn!"

The fact is that during the last few years at least three
of my former colleagues, men of my own generation, have
written and published their memoirs.

Let me hasten to point out that in doing this they were
following an old tradition of the Paris police, to which we
owe, among others, the memoirs of Macé and those of the
great Goron, each in his time chief of what was then called
the Sûreté. As for the most illustrious of them all, Vidocq,
he unfortunately left no recollections written by himself,
which we might compare with the portraits drawn of him
by novelists, often using his name, or else, as in the case
of Balzac, the name Vautrin.

It is not my business to defend my colleagues, but nevertheless I take this opportunity to reply to an objection I have frequently heard raised.

"According to their writings," I have been told, "at least three of them consider themselves responsible for the solution of every famous case."

And people would cite, in particular, the Mestorino case, which was a great sensation in its time.

Now I might make a similar claim myself, because a case of that scope demands the collaboration of every branch of the service. As for the final interrogation—that famous twenty-eight-hour-long interrogation that is cited as an example nowadays—there were not four, but at least six, of us conducting it in shifts, going over the same questions one by one in every conceivable fashion, gaining a little bit of ground each time.

Under these conditions, it would have been hard to say which of us at a given moment had pulled the trigger that provoked a confession.

I wish to assert, moreover, that the title *Memoirs* was not chosen by me, but was finally tacked on because we couldn't think of a better word.

The same is true (I make this point as I correct the proofs) of the subtitles, or what, it seems, are called chapter headings, which the publisher, as an afterthought, asked me to let him add, for typographical reasons, he told me kindly; in actual fact, I suppose, to give a touch of lightness to my text.

Of all the jobs I performed at the Quai des Orfèvres, the only one I ever balked at was the writing of reports. Was this due to an atavistic desire for accuracy, to scruples with which I had seen my father wrestling before me?

The joke has been made so often that it is almost a classic:

"Maigret's reports consist largely of parentheses."

Probably because I try to explain too much, to explain everything, and because nothing seems to me clear or definite.

If the word "memoirs" implies the story of the events in which I have been involved in the course of my career, I'm afraid the public will be disappointed.

In the space of almost half a century I don't think there have been more than a score of really sensational cases, including those to which I have already referred: the Bonnot case, the Mestorino case, plus the Landru case, the Sarrat case, and a few others.

My colleagues, my former chiefs in some cases, have spoken about these at length.

As for the other investigations, those that were interesting in themselves but made no headlines in the newspapers, Simenon has dealt with them.

This brings me to what I wanted to say, what I've been trying to say ever since I started this manuscript, namely, the real justification for these memoirs that are not proper memoirs, and now I know less than ever how I can express myself.

I once read in a paper that Anatole France, who must at least have been an intelligent man and who was fond of indulging in irony, having sat for the painter Van Dongen for his portrait, not only refused to accept the picture once it was finished but forbade it to be shown in public.

It was at about the same period that a famous actress brought a sensational lawsuit against a caricaturist whose portrait of her she thought insulting and injurious to her career.

I am neither an Academician nor a stage star. I don't consider myself to be unduly touchy. Never, during the course of my professional life, have I sent a single correction to the newspapers, although they have never been slow to criticize my activities and my methods.

Nowadays everyone cannot have his portrait painted, but at least we have all had the experience of being photographed. And I suppose everyone is familiar with the discomfort we feel when confronted with a picture of ourselves that is not quite a true likeness.

Is my meaning quite clear? I am rather ashamed of insisting on this. I know I am dealing with a vital, ultrasensitive point, and I feel suddenly afraid of appearing ridiculous, a thing that rarely affects me.

I think I would scarcely mind if I were depicted as a person completely different from what I am, even libelously so.

But let me revert to the comparison with photography. The lens does not permit of complete inaccuracy. The image is different without being different. Faced with the print, you are frequently incapable of putting your finger on the detail that offends you, of saying exactly *what* isn't you, *what* you don't recognize as belonging to yourself.

Well, for years this was my position when faced with Simenon's Maigret, whom I watched growing day by day beside me, so that some people ended by asking me quite seriously whether I had copied his mannerisms, and others whether my name was really my father's name or whether I had borrowed it from the novelist.

I have tried to explain more or less how the thing began, quite innocently, on the whole, and seemingly without importance.

The very youthfulness of the fellow whom worthy Xavier Guichard had introduced to me one day in his office inclined me rather to shrug my shoulders than to harbor suspicions.

And then, a few months later, I was well and truly caught in a mesh from which I have never managed to escape and from which the pages I am now scribbling will not completely rescue me.

"What are you grumbling about? You're famous!"

I know! I know! It's easy to say that when you've not experienced it. I even admit that at certain moments, in certain circumstances, it's not disagreeable. Not merely because it flatters one's vanity. Often for practical reasons. For instance, merely to secure a good seat in a crowded train or restaurant, or to avoid having to wait in line.

For so many years, I never protested, any more than I corrected misstatements in the newspapers.

And I'm not suddenly going to claim that I was boiling inwardly, or chafing at the bit. That would be exaggerating, and I detest exaggeration.

Nonetheless, I promised myself that one day I would say what I want to say, quite quietly, without rancor or ill-feeling, and once and for all put things in their true perspective.

And that day has come.

Why is this book called *Memoirs*? I'm not responsible for that, as I said before, and the word is not of my choosing.

I'm not really concerned here with Mestorino or Landru or with that lawyer in the Massif Central who exterminated his victims by plunging them into a bath full of quicklime.

I'm concerned, more simply, with setting one character against another, one truth against another truth.

You will soon see what some people understand by truth.

It was at the beginning, at the time of that Anthropo-

metrical Ball, which, together with certain other somewhat spectacular affairs in questionable taste, served to
launch what people were already beginning to call "the
first Maigrets," two volumes entitled: *The Hanged Man
of Saint-Pholien* and *The Late Monsieur Gallet*.

Those two, I frankly admit, I read immediately. And I
can still picture Simenon appearing in my office the next
morning, pleased at being himself, even more self-assured
than before, if that were possible, but nonetheless with a
trace of anxiety in his eyes.

"I know what you're going to say to me!" he flung at
me as soon as I opened my mouth.

Pacing up and down, he began to explain:

"I'm quite aware that these books are crammed with
technical inaccuracies. There's no need to count them up.
Let me tell you they're deliberate, and this is why."

I didn't take note of the whole of his speech, but I remember the essential point in it, which he often repeated
to me subsequently with an almost sadistic pleasure:

"Truth never seems true. I don't mean only in literature
or in painting. I won't remind you, either, of those Doric
columns whose lines seem to us strictly perpendicular and
which only give that impression because they are slightly
curved. If they were straight, they'd look as if they were
swelling, don't you see?"

In those days he was still fond of displaying his erudi-
tion.

"Tell someone a story, any story. If you don't dress it
up, it'll seem incredible, artificial. Dress it up, and it'll
seem more real than life."

He trumpeted out those last words as if they implied
some sensational discovery.

"The whole problem is to make something more real

than life. Well, I've done that! I've made you more real than life."

I remained speechless. For a moment I could find nothing to say, poor unreal policeman that I was.

And he proceeded to demonstrate, with an abundance of gestures and the hint of a Belgian accent, that my investigations as told by him were more convincing—he may even have said more accurate—than as experienced by me.

At the time of our first encounters, in the autumn, he had not been lacking in self-confidence. Thanks to success, he was brimming over with it now; he had enough to spare for all the timid folk on earth.

"Follow me carefully, Chief Inspector . . ."

He had decided to drop the "Monsieur."

"In a real investigation there are fifty of you, if not more, busy hunting for the criminal. You and your inspectors aren't alone on the trail. The regular police and the gendarmerie of the whole country are on the alert. They are busy in railroad stations and ports and at frontiers. Not to mention the informers, let alone all the amateurs who offer a hand.

"Just try, in the two hundred or two hundred and fifty pages of a novel, to give a tolerably faithful picture of that swarming activity! A three-decker novel wouldn't be long enough, and the reader would lose heart after a few chapters, mixing up everything, confusing everything.

"Now who is it in real life who prevents this confusion from taking place, who is there every morning putting everyone in his right place and following the guiding thread?"

He looked me up and down triumphantly.

"It's you yourself, as you know very well. It's the man

in charge of the investigation. I'm quite aware that a chief inspector from the Police Judiciaire, the head of a special squad, doesn't roam the streets in person to interview concierges and wine merchants.

"I'm quite aware, too, that, apart from exceptional cases, you don't spend your nights tramping around in the rain through empty streets waiting for some window to light up or some door to open.

"Nonetheless, things happen exactly as if you were there yourself. Isn't that so?"

What could I reply to this? From a certain point of view, it was a logical conclusion.

"So then, let's simplify! The first quality, the essential quality, of truth is to be simple. And I have simplified. I have reduced to their simplest form the wheels within wheels that surround you, without altering the result in the slightest.

"Where fifty more or less anonymous inspectors were swarming in confusion, I have retained only three or four, each with his own personality."

I tried to object:

"The rest won't like it."

"I don't write for a few dozen officials of the Police Judiciaire. When you write a book about schoolteachers, you're bound to offend tens of thousands of schoolteachers. The same would happen if you wrote about stationmasters or typists. What were we talking about?"

"The different kinds of truth."

"I was trying to prove to you that my kind is the only valid one. Would you like another example? One doesn't need to have spent as long as I have in this building to know that the Police Judiciaire, which is part of the Paris police headquarters, can operate only within the perimeter of Paris and, by extension, in certain cases, within the Department of the Seine.

"Now in *The Late Monsieur Gallet* I described an investigation that took place in the middle of France.

"Did you go there, yes or no?"

It was yes, of course.

"I went there, it's true, but at a time when . . ."

"At a period when, for a certain length of time, you were working, not for the Quai des Orfèvres, but for the Rue des Saussaies. Why bother the reader's head with these administrative subtleties?

"Must one begin the account of every case by explaining: 'This took place in such and such a year. So Maigret was attached to such and such a department.'

"Let me finish . . ."

He had his idea and knew that he was about to touch a weak point.

"Are you, in your habits, your attitude, your character, a Quai des Orfèvres man or a Rue des Saussaies man?"

I apologize to my colleagues of the Sûreté Nationale, who include many of my good friends, but I am divulging no secret when I admit that there is, to say the least, a certain rivalry between the two establishments.

Let us admit, too, as Simenon had understood from the beginning, that, particularly in those days, there existed two rather different types of policeman.

Those of the Rue des Saussaies, who are directly answerable to the Ministry of the Interior, are led more or less inevitably to deal with political problems.

I don't blame them for it. I simply confess that, for my own part, I'd rather not be responsible for these.

Our field of action at the Quai des Orfèvres is perhaps more restricted, more down to earth. Our job, in fact, is to cope with malefactors of every sort and, in general, with everything that comes under the heading "police" with the specific limitation "judiciary."

"You'll grant me that you're a Quai des Orfèvres man. You're proud of it. Well, that's what I've made of you; I've tried to make you the incarnation of a Quai des Orfèvres man. And now, for the sake of minutiae, because of your mania for accuracy, have I got to spoil the clarity of the picture by explaining that in such and such a year, for certain complex reasons, you provisionally changed your department, which enabled you to work in any part of France?"

"But . . ."

"One moment. The first day I met you, I told you I was not a journalist but a novelist, and I remember promising Monsieur Guichard that my stories would never involve indiscretions that might prove awkward for the police."

"I know, but . . ."

"Wait a minute, Maigret, for God's sake!"

It was the first time he had called me that. It was the first time, too, that this youngster had told me to be silent.

"I've changed the names, except for yours and those of two or three of your colleagues. I've been careful to change the place names, too. Often, as an extra precaution, I've changed family relationships between the characters.

"I have simplified things, and sometimes I've described only one cross-examination where there were really four or five, and only two or three trails to be followed where, to begin with, you had ten in front of you.

"I maintain that I am in the right, that my truth is the right one.

"I've brought you a proof of it."

He pointed to a pile of books, which he had laid on my desk when he arrived and to which I had paid no attention.

"These are the books written by specialists on matters concerning the police during the last twenty years, true stories, of the kind of truth that you like.

"Read them. For the most part, you're familiar with the investigations these books describe in detail.

"Well I'm willing to bet that you won't recognize them, precisely because the quest for objectivity falsifies that truth which always is and which always *must* be simple.

"And now . . ."

Well! I'd rather admit it right away. That was the moment I realized where the shoe pinched.

He was quite right, of course, on all the points he had mentioned. I didn't worry in the least, either, because he'd reduced the number of inspectors or made me spend nights in the rain in their stead, or because he had, deliberately or not, confused the Sûreté Nationale with the Police Judiciaire.

What shocked me, mainly, although I scarcely liked to admit it to myself, was . . .

Good Lord, how hard this is! Remember what I said about a man and his photograph.

To take merely the detail of the bowler hat. I may appear quite ridiculous, but I must confess that this silly detail hurt me more than all the rest.

When young Sim came to the Quais for the first time, I still had a bowler hat in my closet, but I wore it only on rare occasions, for funerals or official ceremonies.

Now it happened that in my office there hung a photograph taken some years earlier, on the occasion of some conference or other, in which I appeared wearing that cursed hat.

The result is that even today, when I am introduced to people who have never seen me before, I hear them say:

"Why, you're wearing a different hat."

As for the famous overcoat with the velvet collar, it was with my wife that Simenon had to have it out one day, rather than with me.

I did have such a coat, I admit. I even had several, like all men of my generation. It may even have happened that, around 1927, on a day of extreme cold or driving rain, I took down one of those old overcoats.

I'm not a dressy man. I care very little about being elegant. But perhaps for that very reason I have a horror of looking odd. And my little Jewish tailor on Rue de Turenne is no more anxious than I am to have me stared at in the street.

"Is it my fault if that's how I see you?" Simenon might have answered, like the painter who gives his model a crooked nose or a squint.

But in that case the model doesn't have to spend his whole life in front of his portrait, and thousands of people aren't going to believe ever after that he has a crooked nose or a squint.

I didn't tell him all this that morning. I merely averted my eyes and said modestly:

"Was it absolutely necessary to simplify *me*?"

"To begin with, it certainly was. The public has to get used to you, to your figure, your bearing. I've probably hit on the right expression. For the moment you're still only a silhouette, a back, a pipe, a way of talking, of muttering."

"Thanks!"

"The details will appear gradually. You'll see. I don't know how long it will take. Little by little you'll begin to live a more subtle, more complex life."

30

"That's reassuring."

"For instance, up till now, you've had no family life, whereas Boulevard Richard-Lenoir and Madame Maigret actually take up a good half of your existence. You've thus far only telephoned your home, but you're going to be seen there."

"In my dressing gown and slippers?"

"And even in bed."

"I wear nightshirts," I said ironically.

"I know. That completes the picture. Even if you were used to pajamas, I'd have made you wear a nightshirt."

I wonder how this conversation would have ended— probably with a quarrel—if I hadn't been told that a young informer from Rue Pigalle wanted to speak to me.

"On the whole," I said to Simenon, as he held out his hand, "you're pleased with yourself."

"Not yet, but it'll come."

Could I really have announced to him that henceforward I forbade him to use my name? I was legally entitled to do so. And this would have given rise to a typically Parisian lawsuit, which would have covered me with ridicule.

The character would have acquired a different name. But he would still have been me, or, rather, that simplified me who, according to the author, was going to grow progressively more complex.

The worst of it was that the rascal was quite right, and that every month, for years, I was going to find, in a book with a photograph on its cover, a Maigret who imitated me more and more.

If it had been only in books! But the movies were shortly to take it up, and the radio, and, later, television.

It's a strange sensation to watch on the screen, coming and going, speaking and blowing his nose, a fellow who pretends to be you, who borrows certain of your habits, utters sentences that you have uttered, in circumstances that you have known, through which you have lived, in settings that have sometimes been reconstructed with meticulous care.

Actually, the first screen Maigret, Pierre Renoir, was tolerably true to life. I had become a little taller, a little slimmer. The face was different, of course, but certain attitudes were so striking that I suspect the actor of having observed me unawares.

A few months later, I grew some six inches shorter, and what I lost in height I gained in stoutness, becoming, in the shape of Abel Tarride, obese and bland, so flabby that I looked like an inflated rubber animal about to float up to the ceiling. Not to mention the knowing winks with which I underlined my own discoveries and my cunning tricks!

I couldn't sit the film out, and my tribulations were not yet over.

Harry Baur was no doubt a great actor, but he was a full twenty years older than I then was, with a cast of features that was flabby and tragic at the same time.

Let's pass over that!

After growing twenty years older, I suddenly grew almost that much younger again, a good deal later, with a certain Préjean, about whom I have no complaint to make—any more than about the rest of them—but who looked far more like certain young inspectors of the present generation than those of my own.

And finally, quite lately, I have been made to grow stout again, almost to bursting point, and I have begun, in the shape of Charles Laughton, to use English as my native tongue.

Well, of all those, there was one at least who had the

good taste to cheat Simenon and to consider my truth more valid than his.

It was Pierre Renoir, who did not clap a bowler hat on his head, but wore a perfectly ordinary felt hat and the sort of clothes worn by any civil servant, whether or not attached to the police.

I see that I have spoken only of trivial details, a hat, an overcoat—probably because those details were what first shocked me.

You don't feel any surprise at being young first, then at growing old. But let a man so much as cut off the tips of his mustache and he won't recognize himself.

The truth is that I'd like to have finished with what I consider trivial defects before confronting the two characters on essential points.

If Simenon is right, which is quite possible, my own character will appear odd and involved beside that famous simplified—or dressed-up—truth of his, and I will look like some peevish fellow trying to touch up his own portrait.

Now that I've made a beginning, with the subject of dress, I will have to go on, if only for my own peace of mind.

Simenon asked me the other day—actually, he has changed, too, from the young fellow I met in Xavier Guichard's office—he asked me, with a touch of mockery:

"Well, what about the new Maigret?"

I tried to answer him in his former words.

"He's taking shape! He's still nothing but a silhouette. A hat, an overcoat. But it's his real hat. His real overcoat! Little by little, perhaps the rest will come, perhaps he'll have arms and legs and even a face. Who knows? Perhaps he'll even begin to think for himself, without the aid of a novelist."

Actually, Simenon is now just about the age I was when we met for the first time. In those days he tended to think of me as a middle-aged man, and even, in his heart of hearts, as an elderly one.

I did not ask him what he thought about that today, but I couldn't help remarking:

"Do you know that with the course of time you've begun to walk and smoke your pipe and even to speak like *your* Maigret?"

Which is quite true and which, you'll agree, provided me with a rather piquant revenge.

It was rather as if, after all these years, he had begun to take *himself* for *me*!

3

*In which I shall try to talk about a certain
bearded doctor who had some influence on
the life of my family and perhaps, all things
considered, on my choice of a career*

I don't know if I am going to be able to hit the right tone
this time, for I've already filled my wastepaper basket this
morning with the pages I've torn up one after the other.

And last night I almost gave the whole thing up.

While my wife was reading what I had written during
the day, I watched her, pretending to read my paper as
usual, and at a certain point I had the impression that she
was surprised, and from then on to the end she kept
glancing up at me in astonishment and almost in distress.

Instead of speaking to me immediately, she went to put
the manuscript back in the drawer in silence, and it was
some time before she said, trying to keep her remark as
light as possible:

"Anyone would think you didn't like him."

I did not need to ask of whom she was speaking, and it
was my turn to be perplexed, to stare at her in wide-eyed
surprise.

"What are you talking about?" I exclaimed. "Since when has Simenon ceased to be a friend of ours?"

"Yes, of course . . ."

I wondered what could be at the back of her mind, and tried to recollect what I had written.

"I may be mistaken," she added. "Of course I must be mistaken, since you say so. But I had the impression, while reading certain passages, that you felt really resentful about something, and were having your revenge. I don't mean a big, open resentment. Something more secretive, more . . ."

She did not add the word—but I did so for her: ". . . more shameful . . ."

Now Heaven knows how far that was from my mind while I wrote. Not only have I always been on the most cordial terms with Simenon, but he quickly became a friend of the family, and on the few occasions when we have traveled in summer vacations it has almost always been to visit him in his various homes, while he was still living in France: in Alsace, at Porquerolles, in the Charente, the Vendée, and so forth. More recently, when I agreed to go on a semiofficial tour of the United States, it was mainly because I knew I would meet him in Arizona, where he was then living.

"I give you my word . . ." I began gravely.

"I believe you. But perhaps your readers won't."

It's my own fault, I'm convinced. I am not accustomed to using irony, and I realize that I'm probably heavy-handed with it. Whereas I had tried, out of diffidence, to treat this difficult subject with a light touch, since it caused me a certain personal embarrassment.

What I am trying to do, in short, is nothing more or less than to size up one image against another image, one character against its double, rather than against its shadow. And Simenon was the first to encourage me in this undertaking.

I add, to pacify my wife, who is fiercely loyal in her friendships, that Simenon, as I said yesterday in other terms, jokingly, is quite different now from the young man whose aggressive self-confidence occasionally made me wince; that, on the contrary, he is inclined to be taciturn nowadays, and speaks with a certain hesitancy, particularly about any subject on which he feels strongly, is reluctant to make assertions, and, I'd swear, is seeking my approval.

Having said that much, am I to go on teasing him? Just a little, after all. This will be the last time, no doubt. It's too good an opportunity, and I cannot resist it.

In the forty-odd volumes he has devoted to my investigations, there are perhaps a score of references to my origins, to my family, a few words about my father and his profession, estate manager, one mention of the Collège de Nantes, where I was partly educated, and other brief allusions to my two years as a medical student.

And this was the same man who took over four hundred pages to tell the story of his own childhood up to the age of sixteen. It makes no difference that he did so in fictional form, and that his characters may or may not have been true to life; the fact remains that he did not consider his hero complete without the company of his parents and grandparents, his uncles and aunts, whom he describes with all their failings and complaints, their petty vices and their ulcers, while even the neighbor's dog is allotted half a page.

I am not objecting to this, and if I comment on it, it's an indirect way of forestalling any accusation that could be leveled at me of being too long-winded about my own family.

To my mind, a man without a past is not a whole man. In the course of certain investigations, I have sometimes spent more time over the family and background of a suspect than over the suspect himself, and this has often provided the key to what might otherwise have remained a mystery.

It has been said, quite correctly, that I was born in Central France, not far from Moulins, but I don't think it has ever been specified that the estate of which my father was manager was one of seven and a half thousand acres and included no fewer than twenty-six small farms.

Not only was my grandfather, whom I remember, one of these tenant farmers, but he followed at least three generations of Maigrets who had tilled the same soil.

An epidemic of typhus, while my father was still young, had decimated his family, which included seven or eight children, and left only two survivors, my father and a sister, who was later to marry a baker and settle in Nantes.

Why did my father go to the lycée at Moulins, thus breaking with such old traditions? I have reason to believe that the village priest took an interest in him. But it did not mean a break with the land, because, after two years at an agricultural school, he went back to the village and joined the staff at the château as assistant estate manager.

I always feel a certain embarrassment when speaking about him. I have the impression, indeed, that people think: He has retained a child's picture of his parents.

And for a long time I wondered whether possibly I was mistaken, whether my critical sense was not failing me.

But I have had occasion to meet other men of the same type, particularly among those of his generation, mostly from the same social class, which might be described as an intermediary one.

For my grandfather, the family at the château, their

rights, their privileges, their behavior, were not subjects for discussion. What he thought of them in his heart of hearts I never discovered. I was quite young when he died. I'm convinced, nonetheless, when I remember certain looks of his, certain silences particularly, that his approval was not always passive, was not even always approval, nor yet resignation, but that it proceeded, on the contrary, from a certain pride and above all from a highly developed sense of duty.

This was the feeling that persisted in men like my father, mingled with a reserve, a sense of propriety that may have looked like resignation.

I can picture him very well. I have kept some photographs of him. He was very tall, very thin, his thinness emphasized by narrow trousers, bound in by leather gaiters to just below the knee. I always saw my father in leather gaiters. They were a sort of uniform for him. He wore no beard, but a long sandy mustache, in which, when he came home in winter, I used to feel tiny ice crystals when I kissed him.

Our house stood in the courtyard of the château, a pretty house of rose-colored brick, one story high, overlooking the low buildings in which lived several families of farm hands, grooms, and gamekeepers, whose wives for the most part worked at the château as laundresses, needlewomen, or kitchen help.

Within that courtyard my father was a kind of ruler to whom men spoke respectfully, cap in hand.

About once a week he used to drive off at nightfall, sometimes at dusk, with one or more farmers, to go and buy or sell livestock at some distant fair, from which he returned only at the end of the following day.

His office was in a separate building, and on its walls hung photographs of prize oxen and horses, calendars of fairs, and, almost invariably, the finest sheaf of wheat harvested on the estate, shriveling up as the months went by.

About ten o'clock he used to cross the courtyard and go into a private part of the grounds. He would walk around the buildings until he came to the big flight of steps up which the peasants never went, and would then remain closeted for a time within the thick walls of the château.

It was for him, in a word, what our morning conferences are for us at the Police Judiciaire, and as a child I felt proud to see him, very upright, without a trace of servility, as he climbed that awe-inspiring flight of steps.

He spoke little, and he seldom laughed, but when this did happen, it was a surprise to discover how young, almost childish, his laugh was, and to see how much simple pleasantries amused him.

He never drank, unlike most of the people I knew. At each meal a small decanter was set aside for him, half filled with a light white wine made from grapes harvested on the estate, and I never saw him drink anything else, even at weddings and funerals. And at fairs, where he was obliged to stay at inns, he had a cup of his favorite coffee sent up from the kitchen.

I thought of him as a grown man, and even as a middle-aged one. I was five when my grandfather died. As for my mother's parents, they lived over fifty miles away, and we visited them only twice a year, so that I never knew them well. They were not farmers. They kept a grocery in a rather large village, with a café attached to it, as is often the case in country places.

I am not sure, in retrospect, that this was not the reason why our relations with these in-laws were not closer.

I was not quite eight years old when I finally realized that my mother was pregnant. Through remarks overheard by chance, from whispers, I more or less grasped that the thing was unexpected, that after my birth the doctors had declared that she was unlikely to have any more children.

I reconstructed all this later, bit by bit, and I suppose this is always the case with childhood memories.

There was at that time, in the neighboring village, which was bigger than ours, a doctor with a pointed red beard whose name was Gadelle—Victor Gadelle, if I am not mistaken—about whom people talked a great deal, almost always with an air of mystery, and, probably on account of his beard, and also on account of all that was said about him, I was almost inclined to take him for a kind of devil.

There was a drama in his life, a real drama, the first I ever came across and one that impressed me deeply, particularly because it was to have a profound influence on our family, and thereby on my whole existence.

Gadelle drank. He drank more heavily than any peasant in the neighborhood, not only from time to time, but every day, beginning in the morning and only stopping at night. He drank so much that, in a warm room, the atmosphere would be pervaded by a smell of alcohol, which I always sniffed with disgust.

Moreover, he was careless about his person. In fact, you could have called him dirty.

How, under these conditions, could he have been my father's friend? That remained a mystery to me. But the fact is that he often came to see him and talk with him at our home and that there was even a ritual, which consisted of taking out of the glass-fronted cabinet, as soon as he arrived, a small decanter of brandy that was kept for his exclusive use.

About the original drama I knew almost nothing at the

time. Dr. Gadelle's wife had been pregnant, and this must have been for the sixth or seventh time. I thought of her as an old woman already, whereas she was probably about forty.

What had happened on the day of her confinement? Apparently Gadelle came home drunker than usual, and, while waiting to deliver his wife, went on drinking at her bedside.

As it happened, the first stages of her labor were unusually prolonged. The children had been taken to some neighbor's. Toward morning, when nothing seemed to be happening, the sister-in-law who had spent the night at the house went off to see to things at her own home.

Then, apparently, a great noise was heard in the doctor's house, with cries, and footsteps coming and going.

When people got there, they found Gadelle weeping in a corner. His wife was dead. So was the child.

And for a long time after, I would overhear the village gossips whispering in each other's ears, with expressions of indignation or horror:

"A real butchery!"

For months the case of Dr. Gadelle was the main topic of conversation, and, as was to be expected, the neighborhood was split into two factions.

Some people—and there were a good number of them —went into town, which was quite a journey in those days, to consult a different doctor, while others, through indifference or because they still trusted him, went on sending for the bearded doctor.

My father never took me into his confidence on this subject. I am therefore reduced to conjecture.

Gadelle, at any rate, never stopped coming to see us.

He called on us as he had always done, in the course of his rounds, and the familiar gilt-edged decanter was put before him as usual.

He was drinking less, however. People said they never saw him tipsy now. One night he was sent for to the remotest of the farms for a confinement, and he acquitted himself creditably. On his way home he called at our house, and I remember he was very pale; I can still see my father clasping his hand with unwonted persistence, as though to encourage him, as though to tell him: "You see, things weren't so hopeless after all."

For my father never gave up hope as regards people. I never heard him utter an irrevocable judgment, even when the black sheep of the estate, a foul-mouthed farmer of whose malpractices he had had to complain to the landlord, had accused him of some dishonest trick or other.

It is quite certain that if, after the death of Gadelle's wife and child, there had been nobody to stretch out a helping hand to the doctor, he would have been a lost man.

My father did so. And when my mother became pregnant, a certain feeling, which I find it hard to explain, but which I understand, obliged him to see the thing through.

He took precautions, nonetheless. Twice, during the last stage of her pregnancy, he took my mother into Moulins to consult a specialist.

When her time came, a stableboy went on horseback to get the doctor in the middle of the night. I was not sent away from home, but stayed there shut up in my own room, terribly disturbed, although like all country boys I had acquired a certain knowledge of these things at an early age.

My mother died at seven in the morning, as day was

43

breaking, and when I went downstairs, the first thing that caught my eye, in spite of my emotion, was the decanter on the dining-room table.

I was left an only child. A local girl was brought in to look after the house and take care of me. I never saw Dr. Gadelle cross our threshold after that day, but neither did I ever hear my father say one word against him.

A blurred and colorless period followed this drama. I went to the village school. My father spoke less and less. He was thirty-two, and only now do I realize how young that was.

I did not protest when, on completing my twelfth year, I was sent as a boarder to the lycée at Moulins, because it was impossible to take me there every day.

I stayed only a few months. I was unhappy there, a complete stranger in a new world that felt hostile to me. I said nothing about it to my father, who brought me home every Saturday evening. I never complained.

He must have understood, though, because during the Easter vacation his sister, whose husband had opened his bakery in Nantes, suddenly came to see us, and I realized that they were discussing a plan already laid out by letter.

My aunt, whose face was very rosy, had begun to put on weight. She was childless, and this grieved her.

For several days she hovered around me anxiously, telling me about the house in Nantes and its good smell of new bread.

She seemed very cheerful. I had guessed. I was resigned. Or, more precisely, since that's a word I don't care for, I had accepted.

My father and I had a long talk together as we walked through the countryside one Sunday morning after Mass. It was the first time he had talked to me as if I were a man. He was considering my future, the impossibility of studying if I stayed in the village, and if I remained at Moulins as a boarder, the absence of normal family life.

I know now what he was thinking. He had realized that the company of a man like himself, who had withdrawn and lived mainly with his own thoughts, was not desirable for a young boy who still had everything to hope for from life.

I went off with my aunt, a big trunk jolting behind us in the cart that took us to the station.

My father did not shed a tear. Neither did I.

That's more or less all I know about him. For years, in Nantes, I was the nephew of the baker and the baker's wife, and I almost got used to the man I saw every day with his hairy chest glowing in the red light of his oven.

I used to spend all my vacations with my father. I won't go so far as to say we were strangers to one another. But I had my own private life, my ambitions, my problems.

He was my father, whom I loved and respected, but whom I'd given up trying to understand. And it went on like that for years. Is this always the case? I'm inclined to think so.

When my curiosity reawakened, it was too late to ask the questions I so longed to ask then, and I reproached myself for not asking them when he was still there to answer me.

My father had died of pleurisy at the age of forty-four.

I was a young man; I had begun my medical studies. On my last visits to the château, I had been struck by the flush on my father's cheekbones and the feverish glitter of his eyes in the evening.

"Has there ever been any tuberculosis in our family?" I asked my aunt one day.

She said, as though I had spoken of some shameful taint:

"Good heavens, no! All of them were as tough as oak trees! Don't you remember your grandfather?"

I did remember him, precisely. I remembered a certain dry cough, which he put down to smoking. And as far back as I could remember I saw my father with the same cheekbones, under which a fire seemed to be glowing.

My aunt had the same pink flush.

"It's from always living in the heat of a bakery," she would retort.

She died, nonetheless, from the same illness as her brother, ten years later.

As for myself, when I got back to Nantes to collect my belongings before starting on a new life, I hesitated for a long while before calling on one of my professors at his house and asking him to examine me.

"No danger of anything like that," he reassured me.

Two days later I took the train to Paris.

My wife will forgive me this time if I hark back to Simenon and his picture of me, because I want to discuss a point raised by him in one of his latest books, which particularly concerns me.

It is, indeed, one of the points that has irritated me most—and I'm not referring to such petty questions as dress, which I raised as a joke.

I would not be my father's son if I were not somewhat touchy about all that concerns my job, my career—and that's precisely the question.

I have sometimes had an uneasy feeling that Simenon was somehow trying to apologize for me to the public for joining the police. And I am sure that in some people's eyes I only took up this profession as a last resort.

Now it is certainly a fact that I began to study medicine and that I chose that profession of my own free will, without being pushed into it by somewhat ambitious parents, as often happens.

I had not thought about the matter for years, and it had never occurred to me to ask myself any questions about it, when, precisely on account of something that had been written about my vocation, the problem gradually forced itself on me.

I spoke to nobody about it, not even to my wife. Today I have to overcome certain feelings of diffidence to put things in their true light, or try to.

In one of his books, then, Simenon spoke of "a man who mends destinies," and he did not invent the phrase, which was one of my own, which I must have uttered one day when we were chatting together.

Now I wonder if it didn't all spring from Gadelle, whose tragic story, as I subsequently realized, must have made a stronger impression on me than I supposed.

Because he was a doctor, because he had failed, the medical profession had acquired in my eyes an extraordinary prestige; it seemed almost a sort of priesthood.

For years, without realizing it, I had tried to understand the drama of this man fighting a destiny that was too great for him.

And I remembered my father's attitude toward him. I wondered whether my father had understood the same thing I had, whether that was why, at whatever cost to himself, he had let the man try his luck.

From Gadelle I went on gradually to consider most of the people I had known, almost all of them simple folk leading apparently straightforward lives, who nonetheless at one time or another had had to measure themselves against destiny.

Don't forget that I am trying to set down here not the reflections of a mature man, but the workings of a boy's mind, then of an adolescent's.

My mother's death seemed to me so stupid, so *unnecessary*.

And all the other dramatic events I had known, all those failures, had plunged me into a sort of furious despair.

Could nobody do anything about them? I had asked. Might there not be, somewhere, some man wiser or more experienced than the rest—whom I pictured more or less in the shape of a family doctor, of a Gadelle who was not a failure—capable of telling them gently, firmly:

"You're taking a wrong turn. By acting thus you're heading for disaster. Your right place is here rather than there."

I think that was it; I felt dimly that too many people were not in their right places, that they were striving to play parts that were beyond their capacities, so that the game was lost for them before they started.

Above all, please don't imagine that I ever dreamed of becoming that sort of God-the-Father figure myself.

After trying to understand Gadelle, and then to understand my father's attitude toward him, I continued to look around me and ask the same questions.

One example may raise a smile. There were fifty-eight of us in my class one year, fifty-eight pupils with different social backgrounds, different qualities, ambitions, and failings. I had amused myself working out the ideal destiny of all my fellow-pupils and, in my mind, I called them: "the lawyer" . . . "the tax collector" . . .

For quite a while, too, I exercised my wits by guessing what the people I came across would eventually die of.

It is clearer now why I wanted to become a doctor? The word "police," for me, suggested at that time merely the local policeman at the street corner. And if I had heard of the secret police, I had not the least conception what they could be.

And then suddenly I had to earn my living. I arrived in Paris without even the vaguest notion of what career to choose. In view of my unfinished studies, I could at best hope for some office job, and it was with this in mind that, without enthusiasm, I started reading the small ads in the newspapers. My uncle had in vain offered to teach me his trade and keep me at the bakery.

On the same floor of the little hotel where I was living, on the Left Bank, there was a man who aroused my curiosity, a man of about forty who, Heaven knows why, reminded me somewhat of my father.

Physically, indeed, he was as different as possible from the fair, lean, slope-shouldered man whom I had always seen wearing leather gaiters. He was rather short and squat, dark-haired, with a prematurely bald patch which he concealed by carefully combing his hair forward, and black mustaches with curled tips.

He was always neatly dressed in black, wore an overcoat with a velvet collar—which accounts for a certain other overcoat—and carried a stick with a solid silver knob.

I think the likeness to my father lay in his bearing, in a certain way of walking without ever hurrying, of listening, of watching, and then, somehow, of withdrawing within himself.

I met him by chance in a fixed-price restaurant in the neighborhood; I discovered that he took his evening meal there almost every day, and I began, for no definite reason, to want to get to know him.

In vain did I try to guess what his occupation in life might be. He must be unmarried, since he lived alone at the hotel. I used to hear him get up in the morning and come back at night at irregular hours.

He never had any visitors, and the only time I met him with a companion, he was standing at the corner of Boulevard Saint-Michel talking to an individual of such unprepossessing appearance that one might unhesitatingly have described him, at that period, as an "apache."

I was on the point of taking a job with a firm that made passementerie, on Rue des Victoires. I was to call there the next day with references, for which I had written to my former teachers.

That evening at the restaurant, moved by some instinct or other, I decided to rise from my table just as my hotel neighbor was replacing his napkin in his pigeonhole. So I happened to be in place to hold the door open for him.

He must have noticed me before. Perhaps he had guessed that I wanted to speak to him, because he gave me a long look.

"Thank you," he said.

Then, since I was standing still on the sidewalk:

"Are you going back to the hotel?"

"I guess so. . . . I don't know. . . ."

It was a fine late-autumn night. The river was not far off, and the moon could be seen rising behind the trees.

"Alone in Paris?"

"I'm alone, yes."

Without asking for my company, he accepted it, took it for granted as a *fait accompli*.

"You're looking for work?"

"How did you know?"

He did not even bother to answer, just slipped a lozenge between his lips. I was soon to understand why. He was afflicted with bad breath and knew it.

"You're from the provinces?"

"From Nantes, but I come from the country originally."

I spoke freely to him. It was practically the first time since I had come to Paris that I had found a companion, and his silence did not embarrass me at all, no doubt because I was used to my father's friendly silences.

I had told him almost the whole of my story when we found ourselves on Quai des Orfèvres, on the other side of the Pont Saint-Michel.

He stopped in front of a large door that was standing ajar, and said to me:

"Will you wait for me? I'll be only a few minutes."

A policeman in uniform was on duty at the door. After pacing up and down for a while, I asked him:

"Isn't this the Palais de Justice?"

"This is the entrance to the Police Judiciaire."

My hotel neighbor was named Jacquemain. He was in fact unmarried, as I learned that evening while we were walking up and down along the Seine, crossing the same bridges over and over again, with the massive Palais de Justice almost continuously towering over us.

He was a police inspector and he told me about his profession, as briefly as my father would have done about his, with the same underlying pride.

He was killed three years later, before I had myself acquired access to those offices in the Quai des Orfèvres which had come to hold such glamour for me. It happened in the neighborhood of the Porte d'Italie, during a street fight. A bullet, not even intended for him, hit him right in the chest.

His photograph still hangs among the rest in one of those black frames, surmounted by the inscription: "Died in the performance of his duty."

He didn't talk much. He chiefly listened. This did not stop me from asking him, near eleven o'clock that night, in a voice trembling with impatience:

"Do you really think it's possible?"

"I'll give you an answer tomorrow evening."

Of course there was no question of my going straight into the Sûreté. The age of diplomas had not yet arrived, and everyone had to start at the bottom. My only ambition was to be accepted, in any capacity, by one of the Paris police stations, and to be allowed to discover for myself an aspect of the world of which Inspector Jacquemain had merely given me a glimpse.

Just as we were parting on our floor of the hotel, which has since been torn down, he asked:

"Would you very much dislike wearing a uniform?"

I felt a slight shock, I must admit, a brief hesitation, which did not escape his notice and which can scarcely have pleased him.

"No . . ." I replied in a low voice.

And I wore it, though not for long, for seven or eight months. Because I had long legs and was very thin, very quick, strange as that may seem today, they gave me a bicycle and, so that I could get to know Paris, where I was always getting lost, I was given the job of delivering notes to the various police stations.

Has Simenon talked about all this? I don't remember. For months, perched on my bicycle, I threaded my way between carriages and double-decker buses, still horse-drawn, of which I was terribly frightened, particularly when they were tearing down from Montmartre.

Officials still wore frock coats and top hats, and above a certain rank they sported morning coats.

Policemen were mostly middle-aged men with reddish

noses, who were to be seen drinking at bar counters with coachmen and of whom songwriters made relentless fun.

I was unmarried. I felt shy about going courting in my uniform, and I decided that my real life could begin only on the day when I entered the building on Quai des Orfèvres as an inspector, using the main staircase, and not merely as a messenger carrying official notes.

When I mentioned this ambition to my hotel neighbor, he did not smile, but looked at me, musing, and murmured:

"Why not?"

I did not know that I was so soon to attend his funeral. My forecasts about human destiny were still not entirely adequate.

*How I ate petits fours at Anselme and Géraldine's,
thereby shocking Bridges and Highways*

Did my father or my grandfather ever wonder whether
they might have become something other than what they
were? Had they ever had other ambitions? Did they envy
a different lot from their own?

It is strange to have lived with people for so long and
yet to know nothing of what nowadays would seem essential. I have often asked myself the question with the feeling that I was straddling two worlds, totally foreign to one
another.

We talked about it not long ago, Simenon and I, in my
apartment on Boulevard Richard-Lenoir. I think it may
have been on the eve of his departure for the United
States. He had paused to stare at the enlarged photograph
of my father, although he had seen it for years hanging on
the dining-room wall.

While he studied it with particular attention, he kept
casting searching glances at me, as if he were trying to
make comparisons, and this set him pondering.

"The fact is," he finally remarked, "you were born in an ideal milieu, Maigret, at the ideal moment in a family's evolution, to become a top-rank official."

I was struck by this comment, because I had already thought about it, in a less precise and, above all, a less personal way; I had noticed how many of my colleagues came from peasant families, having quite recently lost direct contact with the land.

Simenon went on, almost regretfully and as though he envied me:

"I'm a whole generation ahead of you. I have to go back to my grandfather to find the equivalent of your father. My own father had already reached the civil-servant stage."

My wife was gazing at him attentively, trying to understand, and he added in a lighter tone:

"In the normal course of events I'd have had to make my way up from the bottom in some profession, and work hard to become a doctor or a lawyer or an engineer. Or else . . ."

"Or else what?"

"To become an embittered rebel. Of course that's what usually happens. Otherwise there'd be a plethora of doctors and lawyers. I think I come from the stock that has provided the greatest number of misfits."

I don't know why this conversation has suddenly recurred to me. Probably because I'm recollecting my early years and trying to analyze my frame of mind at that period.

I was all alone in the world. I had just landed in an unfamiliar city in which wealth was flaunted more blatantly than today.

Two things struck one: that wealth, on the one hand,

and that poverty, on the other; and I belonged in the second group.

A whole social set, in full view of the masses, lived a life of sophisticated leisure, and the newspapers reported all the doings of these people who had no other preoccupation than their own pleasures and vanities.

Now not for one moment did I feel tempted to rebel. I did not envy them. I did not hope to be like them one day. I did not contrast my lot with theirs.

For me, they belonged to a world as different from mine as if it had been another planet.

I remember that in those days I had an insatiable appetite, which had already been legendary when I was a child. In Nantes, my aunt often used to tell how she had seen me eat a four-pound loaf when I got back from school, which did not prevent me from having dinner a couple of hours later.

I earned very little money, and my great concern was to satisfy that hunger of mine; I looked for luxury not on the terraces of the famous boulevard cafés, or in the shop windows of Rue de la Paix, but, more prosaically, on pork butchers' counters.

In the streets through which I usually passed, I had discovered a number of pork butchers' shops, which fascinated me, and in the days when I still traveled around Paris in uniform, perched on a bicycle, I used to calculate my time so as to save the few minutes necessary to buy a piece of sausage or a slice of pâté, and devour it, with a roll from the nearby bakery, while standing on the sidewalk outside.

When my stomach was appeased I felt happy and full of self-confidence. I did my job conscientiously. I attached importance to the slightest tasks entrusted to me. And there was no question of overtime. I considered that all of my time belonged to the police, and it seemed to be quite natural that I should be kept at work for fourteen or fifteen hours at a stretch.

If I mention this, it is not that I want to take any credit for it, but, rather, because as far as I can remember it was a common attitude at that time.

Very few policemen had more than a primary education. Through Inspector Jacquemain, the authorities knew —although I myself didn't then know who knew, or even that anyone knew—that I had begun advanced studies. After a few months, I was greatly surprised to find myself appointed to a position I had never dared hope for: that of secretary to the police superintendent of the Saint-Georges district.

And yet the job had an unglamorous name at the time. It was called "being the superintendent's dog."

My bicycle, my cap, and my uniform were taken away from me. So was my chance of stopping at pork butchers' on my way through the Paris streets.

I was particularly grateful for the fact of being in plain clothes one day though, when, walking along Boulevard Saint-Michel, I heard a voice hailing me.

A tall fellow in a white coat was running after me.

"Jubert!" I cried.

"Maigret!"

"What are you doing here?"

"And you?"

"Listen. I can't stop right now. Come and pick me up at seven o'clock in front of the pharmacy."

Jubert, Félix Jubert, was one of my fellow-students at the medical school in Nantes. I knew he had broken off his studies at the same time I did, but, I believe, for different reasons. Without actually being a dunce, he was slow-witted, and I remember they used to say about him:

"He works so hard he breaks out in spots, but he's no wiser next day."

He was very tall and bony, with a big nose, coarse features, red hair, and as long as I'd known him his face had always been covered, not with those small acne pimples that are the bane of young men's lives, but with big red or purple spots, which he spent hours covering with medicated ointments and powders.

I waited for him that same evening at the pharmacy, where he had been working for some weeks. He had no relatives in Paris. He was living in the Cherche-Midi district with people who took in two or three lodgers.

"And what are you doing yourself?"

"I'm in the police."

I can still picture his violet eyes, clear as a girl's, trying to conceal their incredulity. His voice sounded quite odd as he repeated:

"The police?"

He was staring at my suit, instinctively looking for the policeman on duty at the corner of the boulevard, as though to make a comparison.

"I'm secretary to a superintendent."

"Oh, good. I understand."

Whether from conventional pride, or, more likely, because of my inability to explain myself and his inability to understand, I did not confess that three weeks earlier I had still been wearing a uniform, and that my ambition was to join the Sûreté.

In his opinion, and in that of a great many people, a secretary's was a good, respectable job; I sat at a desk, nice and clean, with books in front of me and a pen in my hand.

"Do you have many friends in Paris?"

Apart from Inspector Jacquemain, I really knew nobody, because at the police station I was still new, and they had to watch me before they would make friends with me.

"No girl friend either? What do you do with all your spare time?"

In the first place, I didn't have much of that. And in the second, I spent it studying, because in order to reach my goal faster I had resolved to pass the examinations that had just been instituted.

We ate together that evening. Toward the end of the meal he told me, as if promising me a treat:

"I'll have to introduce you."

"To whom?"

"To some very nice people. Friends of mine. You'll see."

He gave no further explanation that first day. And—I don't know why—it was several weeks before we saw each other again. I might easily never have seen him again. I had not given him my address. I had not asked for his. It never occurred to me to go and wait for him outside the pharmacy.

Chance, once again, brought us face to face at the door of the Théâtre-Français, where we were both waiting in line.

"Isn't it silly," he said. "I thought I'd lost you. I don't even know which police station you're working at. I mentioned you to my friends."

He had a way of talking about these friends that suggested they were a very special set of people, almost a mysterious sect.

"You have a dress suit, I hope?"

"I've got one."

It was pointless to add that it had been my father's

dress suit, which was somewhat old-fashioned, since he had worn it at his wedding, and which I'd had cut to fit me.

"I'll take you there on Friday. You must manage to be free without fail on Friday evening at eight o'clock. Can you dance?"

"No."

"It doesn't matter. But it would be better if you took a few lessons. I know a good school that's not expensive. I've been to it myself."

This time he made a note of my address and even of the little restaurant where I used to have dinner when I was not on duty, and on Friday evening he was in my room, sitting on my bed, while I dressed.

"I must explain to you, so that you don't commit any faux pas. We'll be the only people there, you and I, who aren't connected with the Bridges and Highways Department. A distant cousin of mine, whom I happened to run into, introduced me. Monsieur and Madame Léonard are charming people. Their niece is the loveliest girl in the world."

I gathered at once that he was in love with her and that it was in order to show me the object of his passion that he was dragging me off with him.

"There'll be others; you needn't worry," he promised me. "Very nice girls."

Because it was raining, and we didn't want to arrive covered with mud, we took a carriage, the first I had ever taken in Paris except when on duty. I can still picture our white shirt fronts as we passed under the gas lamps. And I can picture Félix Jubert stopping the cab in front of a florist's shop so that we could decorate our buttonholes.

"Old Monsieur Léonard," he explained, "—Anselme they call him—retired about ten years ago. Before that, he was one of the top officials in the Bridges and High-ways Department, and even now his successors come to consult him sometimes. His niece's father is in Bridges and Highways, too, on the administrative side. And so is all their family, so to speak."

To hear him talk of this government service, you real-ized that for Jubert it was paradise lost, that he would have given anything not to have wasted those precious years studying medicine, so that he, too, could have made a start on such a career.

"You'll see!"

And I saw. It was on Boulevard Beaumarchais, not far from Place de la Bastille, in an oldish but comfortable and fairly well-to-do building. All the windows were lit up on the third floor, and Jubert's upward glance as we got out of the carriage showed me clearly that the party in question was being held there.

I felt rather ill at ease. I began to wish I hadn't come. My stiff collar hurt me; I was convinced that my tie was getting twisted and that one of the tails of my coat tended to curl up like a cock's crest.

The stairway was dimly lit, the steps covered with a crimson carpet that seemed to me sumptuous. And the landing windows were filled with stained glass, which for a long time I considered the last word in refinement.

Jubert had smeared his spotty face with a thicker coat of ointment, which for some reason gave it a purplish sheen. He reverently pulled a big tassel that hung in front of a door. We could hear the buzz of conversation inside, with that touch of shrillness in voices and laughter that suggests the excitement of a social gathering.

A maid in a white apron opened the door to us, and Félix, as he held out his overcoat, was delighted to show himself a regular frequenter of the house by remarking:

"Good evening, Clémence."

"Good evening, Monsieur Félix."

The living room was fairly big, rather dimly lighted, with a great deal of dark upholstery, and in the next room, visible through a wide glass partition, the furniture had been pushed against the wall to leave the floor free for dancing.

With a protective air, Jubert led me up to an old white-haired lady sitting by the fireside.

"May I introduce my friend Maigret, about whom I had the honor of telling you, and who was most anxious to pay you his respects in person."

No doubt he had been rehearsing his sentence all the way there, and was watching to see if I was making a proper bow, did not seem too ill at ease, and, in short, was doing him credit.

The old lady was charming, tiny, with delicate features and a lively expression, but I was disconcerted when she said to me, with a smile:

"Why don't you belong to Bridges and Highways? I'm sure Anselme will be sorry."

Her name was Géraldine. Anselme, her husband, was sitting in another armchair, so still that you would have thought he had been carried in bodily and set down there to be displayed like a waxwork figure. He was very old. I learned later that he was well over eighty and Géraldine just that age.

Somebody was playing the piano softly, a fat youth in a tight coat, while a girl in a pale-blue dress turned the pages for him. I could see her only from the back. When I was introduced to her, I dared not look her in the face, so embarrassed did I feel at being there, not knowing what to say or where to stand.

Dancing had not yet begun. On a small table stood a tray of petits fours, and a little later, since Jubert had left me to my fate, I went up to it—I still don't know why, certainly not out of greed, since I wasn't hungry and I have never liked petits fours; probably to keep my composure.

I took one mechanically. Then a second.

Somebody said, "Hush!"

And a second girl, this time one in a pink dress, with a slight squint, began to sing, standing beside the piano, on which she leaned one hand, waving a fan with the other.

I kept on eating. I was not conscious of it. I was still less conscious that the old lady was watching me with stupefaction, then that others, noticing what I was doing, couldn't take their eyes off me.

One of the young men made some remark to his neighbor and once again somebody said, "Hush!"

You could count the girls by the light-colored patches they made against the men's black coats. There were four of them. Jubert apparently was trying to attract my attention, without success, in great distress at seeing me pick up petits fours one by one and eat them conscientiously. He later admitted that he had felt sorry for me, being convinced I had had no dinner.

Others must have thought the same thing. The song ended. The girl in pink bowed, and everybody clapped; and then I noticed that I was the center of all attention as I stood there beside the little table, my mouth full and a cake in my hand.

I was about to disappear without apologies, to beat a retreat, to run, literally, from that room and that lively crowd that was so totally foreign to me.

Just then, in a shadowy corner, I caught sight of a face,

the face of the girl in blue, and on that face a gentle, reassuring, almost friendly expression. It looked as if she had understood and was encouraging me.

The maid came in with refreshments, but after having eaten so much at the wrong time, I dared not take a glass when it was offered to me.

"Louise, won't you pass the petits fours?"

That was how I learned that the girl in blue was named Louise and also that she was the niece of Monsieur and Madame Léonard.

She waited on everybody before coming up to me, and then, pointing to some cake or other on which there was a small piece of preserved fruit, she said to me with an air of complicity:

"They've left the nicest. Just taste that."

The only answer I could find was:

"Really?"

Those were the first words that passed between Madame Maigret and myself.

Presently, when she reads what I've been writing, I know she'll shrug her shoulders, murmuring:

"What's the good of telling all that?"

Actually, she's delighted with Simenon's picture of her, the picture of a good housewife, always busy cooking and polishing, always fussing over her great baby of a husband. It was even because of that picture, I suspect, that she was the first to become his staunch friend, to the extent of considering him one of the family and of defending him when I haven't dreamed of attacking him.

Now this portrait, like all portraits, is far from being strictly accurate. When I met her on that memorable evening, she was a rather plump young girl with a very fresh face and a sparkle in her eyes that was lacking in her friends'.

What would have happened if I hadn't eaten those cakes? It's quite possible that she would never have noticed me among the dozen or so young men there who all, except my friend Jubert, belonged to Bridges and Highways.

Those three words, "Bridges and Highways," have retained an almost comic significance for us, and if either of us utters them, it makes us both smile; if we hear the words spoken somewhere, we cannot, even now, help casting a knowing glance at one another.

To do things properly I ought to insert here the whole genealogy of the Schöllers, Kurts, and Léonards, which I found most confusing for a long time, and which represents my wife's side of the family.

If you go anywhere in Alsace between Strasbourg and Mulhouse, you will probably hear speak of them. I think it was a Kurt from Scharrachbergheim who first, under Napoleon, founded the almost dynastic tradition of Bridges and Highways. Apparently he was quite famous in his day, and he married into the Schöller family, who were in the same government service.

The Léonards, in their turn, entered the family, and since then, from father to son, from brother to brother-in-law or cousin, practically everybody has belonged to the same organization, to such an extent that it was considered a comedown for a Kurt to become one of the biggest brewers in Colmar.

I only guessed some of this on that first evening, thanks to the few hints that Jubert had given me.

And when we went out into the driving rain, not bothering this time to take a carriage, which, in any case, we would have had difficulty finding in that district, I had almost begun to feel, regretfully, that I'd chosen the wrong career myself.

"What d'you think of that?"

"Oh what?"

"Of what Louise did! I'm not going to reproach you. But it was a very awkward situation. Did you see how tactfully she put you at your ease, without showing it? She's an amazing girl. Alice Perret may be more brilliant, but . . ."

I didn't know who Alice Perret was. The only person who had made any impression on me that whole evening was the girl in pale blue, who, between dances, had come to chat with me.

"Alice is the one who sang. I think she's going to get engaged to the boy who came with her, Louis, whose parents are very rich."

We parted very late that night. At every new downpour we went into some bistro that was still open, to take shelter and drink a cup of coffee. Félix would not let me go, talking unceasingly about Louise, trying to make me admit that she was the ideal girl.

"I know I don't stand much chance. It's because her parents want to find her a husband in Bridges and Highways that they've sent her to stay with her uncle Léonard. You see, there are no more available in Colmar or in Mulhouse, or else they're in the family already. She's been here two months now. She is to spend the whole winter in Paris."

"Does she know?"

"What?"

"That she's supposed to marry into Bridges and Highways."

"Of course. But she doesn't care. She's a most independent girl, far more than you might think. You didn't have time to appreciate her. Next Friday you must try to talk to her more. If you could dance, it would make things easier. Why don't you take two or three lessons in the meantime?"

I took no dancing lessons. Which was just as well. For Louise, contrary to the worthy Jubert's belief, disliked nothing so much as gliding around in the arms of a dancing partner.

Two weeks later, a trivial incident occurred, which, at the time, seemed of great moment to me—and which perhaps was, but in a different way.

The young engineers who used to visit the Léonards were an exclusive clique and they affected the use of words that had no meaning for anyone outside their own set.

Did I detest them? Most likely. And I objected to their insistent habit of calling me "the Police Inspector." It had become a tiresome game.

"Well, Inspector . . ." they would call to me from one end of the room to the other.

Now, that particular evening, while Jubert and Louise were chatting in one corner, close to a green plant I can still picture, a young man in glasses went up and whispered something to them, with a laughing glance in my direction.

A few minutes later I asked my friend:

"What was he saying?"

Visibly embarrassed, he said evasively:

"Nothing."

"Something spiteful?"

"I'll tell you when we've left."

The boy with glasses repeated his performance with other groups, and everybody seemed to be having a good laugh at my expense.

Everybody except Louise, who refused a good many dances that evening and spent the time talking to me.

Once outside, I questioned Félix.

"What did he say?"

"Tell me frankly first: What did you do before you became the superintendent's secretary?"

"Well . . . I was in the police. . . ."

"In uniform?"

So that was the great sensation. The spectacled fellow must have recognized me from having seen me in my policeman's outfit.

Just imagine a policeman among the gentlemen from Bridges and Highways!

"What did she say?" I asked, with a lump in my throat.

"She was wonderful. She's always wonderful. You won't believe me, but you'll see. . . ."

Poor old Jubert!

"She told him that you must certainly have looked better in uniform than he would."

Nevertheless, I stayed away from Boulevard Beaumarchais the following Friday. I avoided meeting Jubert. Two weeks or so later, he came himself to hunt for me.

"Well, they were asking after you on Friday."

"Who was?"

"Madame Léonard. She asked me if you were ill."

"I've been very busy."

I felt sure that if Madame Léonard had spoken of me, it was because of her niece. . . .

Well! I don't think there is any point in going into all the details. It's going to be hard enough to make sure that what I've written already doesn't get thrown into the wastepaper basket.

For nearly three months, Jubert played his part without suspecting anything, and, indeed, without our making any effort to deceive him. It was he who used to come and get me at my hotel and tie my bow tie for me on the pretext that I didn't know how to dress. It was he, also, who used to tell me when he saw me sitting by myself:

"You ought to pay some attention to Louise. You're not being polite."

And when we left, it was always he who insisted:

"You're quite wrong to suppose that she's not interested in you. On the contrary, she's very fond of you. She's always asking me about you."

Toward Christmas, the girl friend with the squint got engaged to the pianist, and they stopped coming to Boulevard Beaumarchais.

I don't know if Louise's attitude was beginning to discourage the rest, if we were perhaps less discreet than we imagined. The fact remains that there were gradually fewer guests each Friday at Anselme and Géraldine's.

Jubert finally had it out with me in February, in my room. That Friday, he was not wearing evening dress, as I noticed immediately. He had the look of resigned bitterness of some of the great roles at the Comédie-Française.

"I've come to tie your bow tie, in spite of everything!" he said with a forced smile.

"You're not free tonight?"

"On the contrary, I'm completely free, free as the air, freer than I've ever been."

And standing before me with my white tie in his hand, and his eyes boring into mine:

"Louise has told me everything."

I was dumbfounded. For so far she'd told *me* nothing. And I had told her nothing, either.

"What are you talking about?"

"About you and her."

"But . . ."

"I put the question to her. I went to see her on purpose yesterday."

"But what question?"

"I asked her if she would marry me."

"And she said no?"

"She said no, that she was very fond of me, that I would always be her best friend, but that . . ."

"Did she mention me?"

"Not exactly."

"Well then?"

"I've understood! I ought to have understood that first evening, when you ate those petits fours and she looked at you indulgently. When a woman looks so indulgently at a man who's behaving as you were . . ."

Poor Jubert! We lost sight of him almost immediately, just as we lost sight of all the Bridges and Highways gentlemen, apart from Uncle Léonard.

For years we never knew what had become of him. And I was getting on toward fifty when one day, on the Canebière in Marseilles, I went into a pharmacy to buy some aspirin. I hadn't read the name on the front. I heard an exclamation:

"Maigret!"

"Jubert!"

"What's been happening to you? Silly of me to ask, since I've known all about you from the newspapers for a long time. How is Louise?"

Then he told me about his eldest son, who, by a nice

irony of fate, was preparing for the Bridges and Highways examination.

With Jubert missing from Boulevard Beaumarchais, the Friday soirées became even more sparsely attended, and often, now, there was nobody to play the piano. On such occasions, Louise would play and I would turn the pages for her, while one or two couples danced in the dining room, which had now grown too big.

I don't think I asked Louise if she was willing to marry me. Most of the time we talked about my career, about the police, about an inspector's job.

I told her how much I would earn when I was at last appointed to the Quai des Orfèvres, adding that this would take at least three years and that until then my salary would hardly be adequate to set up house properly.

I told her, too, about the two or three interviews I had had with Xavier Guichard, who was already our Big Chief, and who had not forgotten my father and had more or less taken me under his wing.

"I don't know if you like Paris. Because, you see, I will have to spend all my life in Paris."

"You can live here as quietly as in the provinces, can't you?"

Finally, one Friday, I found no guests there, only Géraldine, who came to open the door for me herself, in her black silk dress, and who said to me in a rather solemn voice:

"Come in!"

Louise was not in the living room. There were no trays of cakes and no refreshments. Spring had come, and there was no fire burning on the hearth. I felt I had nothing to cling to, and I had kept my hat in my hand, ill at ease in my dress suit and patent-leather pumps.

"Tell me, young man, what are your intentions?"

That was probably one of the most painful moments in my life. The voice sounded to me hard and accusing. I dared not raise my eyes, and I could see nothing but the edge of a black dress against the flower-patterned carpet, with the tip of a very pointed shoe showing. My ears turned scarlet.

"I swear . . ." I stammered.

"I'm not asking you to swear, I'm asking you if you intend to marry her."

I looked at her at last, and I don't think I have ever seen an old woman's face expressing so much affectionate mischief.

"But of course!"

Apparently—I've been told so often enough since—I jumped up like a jack-in-the-box and repeated, still louder:

"Of course!"

And I almost shouted a third time:

"Why, of course!"

She did not even raise her voice to call:

"Louise!"

And Louise, who was standing behind a half-open door, came in awkwardly, blushing as much as I was.

"What did I tell you?" said her aunt.

"Why?" I broke in. "Didn't she believe it?"

"I wasn't sure. It was Auntie . . ."

Let us skip the next scene, for I'm sure my wife would censor it.

Old Léonard, for his part, showed much less enthusiasm, I must admit, and he never forgave me for not belonging to Bridges and Highways. He was very old, almost a centenarian, and riveted to his armchair by his infirmities; he would look at me and shake his head, as if something had gone badly wrong with the way of the world.

"You'll have to take leave to visit Colmar. What about the Easter holiday?"

Old Géraldine wrote to Louise's parents, a series of letters—to prepare them for the shock, she said—breaking the news to them.

At Easter I was allowed barely forty-eight hours' leave. I spent most of it in trains, which were less rapid then than today.

I was given a perfectly proper reception, without wild enthusiasm.

"The best way to find out if both of you are serious is to stay away from one another for some time. Louise will spend the summer here. In the autumn you can come back to see us."

"May I write to her?"

"Within reason. Once a week, for instance."

It seems funny today. It was not at all funny at the time.

I had promised myself, without a trace of secret spite, to choose Jubert as best man. When I went to find him at the pharmacy on Boulevard Saint-Michel, he had left, and nobody knew what had become of him.

I spent part of the summer hunting for an apartment, and I found this one on Boulevard Richard-Lenoir.

"Until we find something better, you understand? When I'm promoted to inspector . . ."

Dealing somewhat haphazardly with
hobnailed socks, apaches, prostitutes,
radiators, sidewalks, and railroad stations

A few years ago some of us talked of founding a sort of club, more likely a monthly dinner, which was to be called "The Hobnailed Socks Club." We got together for a drink, in any case, at the Brasserie Dauphine. We argued about who should and who shouldn't be admitted. And we wondered quite seriously whether those from the other branch, I mean from the Rue des Saussaies, should be considered eligible.

Then, as was only to be expected, things went no further. At that time there were still at least four of us, among the inspectors of the Police Judiciaire, who were rather proud of the nickname "hobnailed socks," given to us once upon a time by satirical songwriters, and which certain young inspectors fresh from college sometimes used among themselves when referring to those of their seniors who had risen from the ranks.

In the old days, indeed, it took a good many years to

win one's stripes, and exams were not enough. An inspector, before hoping for promotion, had to have worn out his shoe soles in practically every branch of the service.

It is not easy to convey the meaning of this with any sort of precision to the younger generation.

"Hobnailed shoes" and "big mustaches" were the terms that sprang naturally to people's lips when they spoke of the police.

And, in fact, for years I wore hobnailed shoes myself. Not from choice. Not, as caricaturists seemed to imply, because we thought such footwear was the height of elegance and comfort, but for more down-to-earth reasons.

Two reasons, to be exact. The first was that our salary barely enabled us to make ends meet. I often hear people talk of the gay, carefree life at the beginning of this century. Young people refer enviously to the prices current at that time, cigars at two sous, dinner with wine and coffee for twenty sous.

What people forget is that at the outset of his career a public servant earned somewhat under a hundred francs a month.

When I was a foot patrolman, I would cover during my day, which was often thirteen or fourteen hours, miles and miles of sidewalk, in all kinds of weather.

So that one of the first problems of our married life was the problem of getting my shoes soled. At the end of each month, when I brought my pay envelope to my wife, she would divide its contents into a number of small piles.

"For the butcher . . . For rent . . . For gas . . ."

There was hardly anything left to put in the last pile of small change.

"For your shoes."

75

Our dream was always to buy new ones, but for a long time it was only a dream. Often I went for weeks without confessing to her that my soles, between the hobnails, absorbed the gutter water greedily.

If I mention this here it is not out of bitterness but, on the contrary, quite light-heartedly, because I think it is necessary to give an idea of a policeman's life.

There were no such things as taxis, and even if the streets had been crowded with them, they would have been beyond our reach, as were the cheaper carriages, which we used only in very special circumstances.

Besides, in the Public Roads Squad, our duty was to keep walking along the sidewalks, mingling with the crowd from morning till night and from night until morning.

Why, when I think of those days, do I chiefly remember the rain? As if it had rained unceasingly for years, as if the seasons were different then. Of course, it is because the rain added a number of additional ordeals to one's job. Not only did your socks become soaked, but the shoulders of your coat gradually turned into cold compresses, your hat became a waterspout, and your hands, thrust into your coat pockets, grew blue with cold.

The streets were less well lighted than they are today. A certain number of them in the outskirts were unpaved. At night the windows showed as yellowish squares against the blackness, for most of the houses were still lighted by oil lamps or even, more wretched still, by candles.

And then there were the apaches.

All around the fortifications, in those days, their knives would come into play, and not always for gain, for the sake of a rich man's wallet or watch.

What they wanted chiefly was to prove to themselves

that they were men, "tough guys," and to win the admiration of the little tarts in black pleated skirts and huge chignons who paced the sidewalks under the gas jets.

We were unarmed. Contrary to the general belief, a policeman in plain clothes does not have the right to carry a revolver in his pocket, and if, in certain cases, a man takes one, it's against the regulations and entirely on his own responsibility.

Junior officers could never consider themselves entitled to do so. There were a certain number of streets, in the neighborhood of La Villette, Ménilmontant, and the Porte d'Italie, where one ventured reluctantly and sometimes trembled at the sound of one's own footsteps.

For a long time, a telephone remained a legendary luxury beyond the scope of our budgets. When I was delayed several hours, there was no question of calling my wife to warn her; so she used to spend lonely evenings in our gas-lit dining room, listening for noises on the staircase and warming up the same dish four or five times over.

As for the mustaches with which we were caricatured, we really wore them. A man without a mustache looked like a flunky.

Mine was longish, reddish brown, somewhat darker than my father's, with pointed ends. Later it dwindled to a toothbrush, and then disappeared completely.

It is a fact, moreover, that most police inspectors wore huge jet-black mustaches like those in their caricatures. This is because, for some mysterious reason, for quite a long time the profession mostly attracted natives of the Massif Central.

There are few streets in Paris along which I have not trudged, eyes watchful, and I learned to know all the street people, from beggars, organ grinders, and flower girls to cardsharps and pickpockets, including prostitutes and the drunken old women who spend most of their nights at the police station.

I "covered" the Halles at night, Place Maubert, the quays and underneath the quays.

I "covered" the crowds, too, the biggest job of all, at the fairs at Trône and Neuilly, at Longchamps races and patriotic demonstrations, at military parades, visits from foreign royalty, carriage processions, traveling circuses, and flea markets.

After a few months, a few years at this job, one's head is full of a varied array of figures and faces, which remain indelibly engraved on one's memory.

I would like to try—although it's not easy—to give a more or less accurate idea of our relations with these people, including those whom we periodically had to take off to the lockup.

Needless to say, the picturesque aspect soon ceases to exist for us. Inevitably, we come to scan the streets of Paris with a professional eye, which fastens on certain familiar details or notices some unusual circumstance and draws the necessary conclusion from it.

When I consider this subject, the thing that strikes me most is the bond that is formed between the policeman and the quarry he has to track down. Above all, except in a few exceptional cases, the policeman is entirely devoid of hatred or even of ill will.

Devoid of pity, too, in the usual sense of the word.

Our relations are, so to speak, strictly professional.

We have seen too much, as you can well imagine, to be shocked any longer by certain forms of wretchedness and depravity. So the latter does not arouse our indignation, nor does the former cause us the distress felt by the inexperienced spectator.

There is something between us, which Simenon has tried to convey without success, and that is, paradoxical as it may seem, a kind of family feeling.

Don't misunderstand me. We are on different sides of the barricade, of course. But we also, to some extent, share the same hardships.

The prostitute on Boulevard de Clichy and the policeman who is watching her both have had shoes and both have aching feet from trudging along miles of asphalt. They have to endure the same rain, the same icy wind. Evening and night wear the same hue for both of them, and they see with almost identical eyes the seamy side of the crowd that streams past them.

The same is true of a fair where a pickpocket is threading his way through a similar crowd. For him a fair, or indeed any gathering of a few hundred people, means, not fun, merry-go-rounds, circus tents, or gingerbread, but merely a certain number of purses in unwary pockets.

For the policeman, too. And each of them can recognize at a glance the self-satisfied country visitor who will be the ideal victim.

How many times have I spent hours following a certain pickpocket of my acquaintance, such as the one we called "the Dodger"! He knew that I was on his heels, watching his slightest movements. And I knew that he knew that I was there.

His job was to get hold of a wallet or a watch in spite of it, and my job was to stop him or catch him in the act.

Well, it sometimes happened that the Dodger would turn around and smile at me. I would smile back. He even spoke to me sometimes, with a sigh:

"It's going to be hard!"

I was well aware that he was on his beam-ends and that he wouldn't eat that night unless he was successful.

He was equally well aware that I earned a hundred francs a month, that I had holes in my shoes, and that my wife was waiting impatiently for me at home.

Ten times at least I picked him up, quite kindly, telling him:

"You've had it!"

And he was almost as relieved as I was. It meant that he'd get something to eat at the police station and somewhere to sleep. Some of them know the lockup so well that they ask:

"Who's on duty tonight?"

Because some of us let them smoke and others don't.

Then, for a year and a half, the streets seemed to me an ideal beat, because my next job was in the big stores.

Instead of rain and cold, sunshine and dust, I spent my days in an overheated atmosphere reeking of tweed and unbleached cotton, linoleum, and mercerized thread.

In those days there were radiators at intervals in the aisles between counters, which sent up puffs of dry, scorching air. This was fine when you arrived soaking wet. You took up your position near a radiator, and immediately you gave out a cloud of steam.

After a few hours, you chose instead to hang around near the doors, which, each time they opened, let in a little oxygen.

The important thing was to look natural. To look like a customer! Which is so easy, isn't it, when the whole floor is full of nothing but corsets, lingerie, or bolts of silk?

"May I ask you to come along with me quietly?"

Some women used to understand immediately and followed us without a word to the manager's office. Others got on their high horse, protested shrilly, or had hysterics.

And yet here, too, we had to deal with a regular clientele. Whether at Bon Marché, the Louvre, or Printemps,

80

certain familiar figures were always to be found, usually middle-aged women, who stowed away incredible quantities of various goods in a pocket concealed between their dress and their petticoat.

A year and a half, in retrospect, seems very little, but at the time, each hour was as long drawn out as an hour spent in the dentist's waiting room.

"Will you be at the Galeries this afternoon?" my wife would ask me sometimes. "I have a few things to buy there."

We never spoke to one another. We pretended not to recognize each other. It was delightful. I was happy to watch her moving proudly from one counter to the next, giving me a discreet wink from time to time.

I don't believe that she ever asked herself whether she might have married someone other than a police inspector. She knew the names of all my colleagues, spoke familiarly about those whom she had never seen, of their hobbies, of their successes or their failures.

It took me years to bring myself, one Sunday morning when I was on duty, to take her into the famous building on Quai des Orfèvres, and she showed no sign of wonder. She walked around as if she were at home, looking for all the details she knew so well from hearsay.

Her only reaction was:

"It's less dirty than I'd expected."

"Why should it be dirty?"

"Places where men live by themselves are never quite clean. And they have a certain smell."

I did not ask her to a police station, where she'd have got her fill of smells.

"Who sits here on the left?"

"Torrence."

"The big fat one? I might have guessed. He's like a

child. He still amuses himself by carving his initials in the desk.

"And what about Old Lagrume, the man who walks so much?"

Since I've talked about shoes, I may as well tell the story that distressed my wife.

Lagrume, Old Lagrume, as we called him, was senior to all of us, although he had never risen to the rank of inspector. He was a tall, melancholy man. In summer he suffered from hay fever, and as soon as the weather turned cold, his chronic bronchitis gave him a hollow cough that sounded from one end to the other of the Police Judiciaire.

Fortunately, he was not often there. He had been rash enough to say one day, referring to his cough:

"The doctor recommends that I keep in the open air."

After that, he got his fill of open air. He had long legs and huge feet, and he was put in charge of the most unlikely investigations through the length and breadth of Paris, the sort that force you to travel through the city in all directions, day after day, without even the hope of getting any results.

"Just leave it to Lagrume!"

Everybody knew what was involved, except the good-natured old man himself, who gravely made a few notes in his book, tucked his rolled umbrella under his arm, and went off, after a brief nod to everybody there.

I wonder now whether he was not perfectly well aware of the part he was playing. He was one of the meek. For years and years he had had a sick wife waiting for him to do the housework in their home in the suburbs. And after his daughter married, I believe it was he who got up at night to look after the baby.

"Lagrume, you still smell of dirty diapers!"

An old woman had been murdered on Rue Caulain-court. It was a commonplace crime, which made no noise in the press, for the victim was an unimportant owner of a small income, and had no connections.

Such cases are always the most difficult. I myself, being confined to the big stores—and particularly busy as Christmas drew near—was not involved in it, but, like everybody else in our building, I knew the details of the investigation.

The crime had been committed with a kitchen knife, which had been left on the spot. This knife provided the only evidence. It was quite an ordinary knife, such as are sold in hardware and general stores, even the smallest local shops, and the manufacturer, who had been found, claimed to have sold tens of thousands within the Paris area.

The knife was a new one. It had obviously been bought on purpose. It still had the price written on the handle in indelible pencil.

This was the detail that offered a vague hope of dis-covering the shopkeeper who had sold it.

"Lagrume! You deal with that knife."

He wrapped it up in a piece of newspaper, put it in his pocket, and set off.

He set off for a journey through Paris that was to last for nine weeks.

Every morning he appeared punctually at the office, to which he would return in the evening to shut the knife away in a drawer. Every morning he was to be seen put-ting the weapon in his pocket, seizing his umbrella, and setting out with the same nod to everybody there.

I learned the number of shops—the story has become a legend—that might possibly have sold a knife of this kind. Without going beyond the fortifications, and confining oneself to the twenty arrondissements of Paris, the number makes your head reel.

There was no question of using any means of transport. It meant going from street to street, almost from door to door. Lagrume had in his pocket a map of Paris, on which, hour after hour, he crossed out a certain number of streets.

I believe that in the end his chiefs had even forgotten what job he'd been given.

"Is Lagrume available?"

Somebody would reply that he was out on a job, and then nobody bothered any more about him. It was shortly before Christmas, as I have said. It was a wet, cold winter, the sidewalks were slimy, and yet Lagrume went back and forth from morning till night, with his bronchitis and his hollow cough, unwearying, never asking what was the point of it all.

During the ninth week, well into the New Year, when it was freezing hard, he turned up at three o'clock in the afternoon, as calm and mournful as ever, without the slightest gleam of joy or relief in his eyes.

"Is the Chief here?"

"You've found it?"

"I've found it."

Not in a hardware store, or a general store, or a household-goods shop. He had gone through all those in vain.

The knife had been sold by a stationer on Boulevard Rochechouart. The shopkeeper had recognized his handwriting, and remembered a young man with a green scarf buying the weapon from him more than two months ago.

He gave a fairly detailed description of him, and the young man was arrested and executed the following year.

As for Lagrume, he died in the street, not from his bronchitis, but from a heart attack.

• • •

Before discussing stations, and in particular that Gare du Nord with which I always feel I have an old score to settle, I must deal briefly with a subject of which I am not very fond.

I have often been asked, with reference to my early days and my various jobs:

"Have you been in the Vice Squad, too?"

It isn't known by that name today. It is modestly called the "Morals Squad."

Well, I have belonged to that, like most of my colleagues. For a very short period. Only a few months.

And, although I realize now that it was necessary, my recollections of that period are nevertheless vague and somewhat uneasy.

I mentioned the familiarity that grows up naturally between policemen and those on whom it is their job to keep watch.

By force of circumstances, it exists in that branch of the service as much as in the others. Even more so. Indeed, the "clientele" of each inspector, so to speak, consists of a relatively restricted number of women who are almost always found at the same spots, at the door of the same hotel or under the same street lamp, or, for the level above, on the terrace of the same brasseries.

I was not then as broad as I have grown with the passing years, and apparently I looked younger than my age.

Remember the petits fours incident on Boulevard Beaumarchais and you will understand that in certain respects I was somewhat timid.

Most of the officers in the Vice Squad were on familiar terms with the women, whose names or nicknames they knew, and it was a tradition, when, during the course of a raid, they packed them into the Black Maria, to vie with them in coarseness of speech, to fling the filthiest abuse at each other with a laugh.

Another habit these women had acquired was to pick up their skirts and show their behinds, in a gesture they considered, no doubt, the last word in insults, and which they accompanied with a torrent of defiance.

I must have blushed in the beginning, for I still blushed easily. My embarrassment did not pass unnoticed, since the least one can say of these women is that they have a certain knowledge of men.

I promptly became, not exactly their *bête noire*, but their butt.

At the Quai des Orfèvres nobody ever called me by my first name, and I'm convinced that many of my colleagues did not know it. . . . I wouldn't have chosen it if I'd been asked my opinion, but I'm not ashamed of it either.

Could it have been some sly revenge on the part of some inspector who was in the know?

I was especially in charge of the Sébastopol district, which, particularly in the Halles area, was frequented at that time by the lowest class of women, particularly by a number of very old prostitutes who had taken refuge there.

It was there, too, that young servant girls newly arrived from Brittany or elsewhere served their apprenticeship, so that one had the two extremes: gamines of sixteen, over whom the pimps quarreled, and ancient harpies, who were very well able to defend themselves.

One day the joke started—for the catchphrase quickly became a joke. I was walking past one of these old women, stationed at the door of a sordid hotel, when I heard her call out to me, showing all her rotten teeth in a smile:

"Good evening, Jules!"

I thought she'd used the name at random, but a little farther on I was greeted by almost the same words.

"Hello, Jules!"

After which, when there was a group of them together, they would burst out laughing, and utter a flood of unrepeatable comments.

I know what some of my colleagues would have done in my place. They would have needed no further inducement to pick up a few of these women and lock them up in Saint-Lazare to think things over.

The example would have served its purpose, and I would probably have been treated with a certain respect.

I didn't do it. Not necessarily from any sense of justice. Nor out of pity.

Probably because this was a game I didn't want to play. I chose, instead, to pretend I hadn't heard. I hoped they would grow tired of it. But such women are like children, who never have enough of any joke.

They made up a song about Jules, which they began to sing or yell as soon as I appeared. Others would say to me, as I checked their cards:

"Don't be mean, Jules! You're so sweet!"

Poor Louise! Her great dread, during this period, was, not that I might yield to some temptation, but that I might bring home an unpleasant disease. Once, I caught fleas. When I got home, she would make me undress and take a bath, while she brushed my clothes out in the hall or at the open window.

"You must have touched plenty today! Brush your nails well!"

Wasn't there some story that you could catch syphilis merely by drinking out of a glass?

It was not a pleasant experience, but I learned what I had to learn. After all, I had chosen my career.

For nothing on earth would I have asked to be transferred. My chiefs did what was necessary of their own accord, more for the sake of results, I imagine, than out of consideration for me.

I was assigned to stations. More precisely, I was posted to that gloomy, sinister building known as the Gare du Nord.

It had the advantage, like the big stores, that one was sheltered from the rain. Not from the cold or from the wind, because nowhere in the world, probably, are there so many drafts as in the main room of a station, the main room of the Gare du Nord, and for months I had as many colds as old Lagrume.

Please don't imagine that I am sorry for myself, or deliberately dwelling on the seamy side for reasons of revenge.

I was perfectly happy. I was happy trudging along the streets and equally so keeping an eye on so-called kleptomaniacs in the big stores. I felt that I was getting along a little each time, learning a job whose complexity was more apparent to me every day.

When I see the Gare de l'Est, for instance, I can never help feeling depressed, because it reminds me of mobilization. The Gare de Lyon, on the other hand, like the Gare Montparnasse, suggests vacations.

But the Gare du Nord, the coldest, the busiest of them all, brings to my mind a harsh and bitter struggle for one's daily bread. Is it because it leads toward mining and industrial regions?

In the morning, the first night trains, coming from Belgium and Germany, generally contain a certain number of smugglers, of illicit dealers, with faces as hard as the daylight seen through the windows of the station.

It is not always a matter of small-scale fraud. There are the professionals in various international rackets, with their agents, their front men, their right-hand men, people who play for high stakes and are ready to defend themselves by any method.

No sooner has this crowd dispersed than it's the turn of the suburban trains, which come, not from pleasant villages like those in the west or south, but from black, unhealthy built-up areas.

In the opposite direction, it's toward Belgium, the nearest frontier, that fugitives for the most varied reasons try to escape.

Hundreds of people are waiting there in the gloom redolent of smoke and sweat, moving restlessly, hurrying from the ticket windows to the waiting rooms, examining the boards that announce arrivals and departures, eating or drinking, surrounded by children, dogs, and suitcases, and almost always they are people who have not slept enough, whose nerves are on edge from their fear of being late, sometimes merely from their dread of the morrow they are going elsewhere to seek.

I have spent hours, entire days, watching them, looking among all those faces for some more inscrutable face, with a more fixed stare, the face of a man or woman staking everything on their last chance.

The train is there, about to leave in a few minutes. He's only got to go another hundred yards and hold out the ticket he's clutching. The minute hands jerk forward on the enormous yellowish face of the clock.

Double or nothing! It means freedom or jail. Or worse.

I am there, with a photograph or a description in my wallet, sometimes merely the technical description of an ear.

It may happen that we catch sight of one another

simultaneously, that our eyes meet. Almost invariably the man understands at once.

What follows will depend on his character, on the risk he's running, on his nerves, even on some tiny material detail, a door that's open or shut, a trunk that may happen to be lying between us.

Sometimes he tries to run away, and then there's a desperate race through groups of people who protest or try to get out of the way, a race through stationary coaches, over tracks and switches.

I have come across two men, one of them quite young, who, three months apart, behaved in exactly the same way.

Each of them thrust his hand into his pocket as if to take out a cigarette. And the next minute, in the thick of the crowd, with his eyes fixed on me, each shot himself through the head.

These men bore me no ill will, nor did I bear them any.

We were each doing his job.

They had lost the game, and that was that, so they were getting out.

I had lost it, too, because my duty was to bring them to justice alive.

I have watched thousands of trains leaving. I have watched thousands arriving, too, each time with the same dense crowd, the long string of people hurrying toward something or other.

It has become a habit with me, as with my colleagues. Even if I'm not on duty, if by some miracle I'm going on a vacation with my wife, my glance slips from one face to the next, and seldom fails to fall on somebody who's afraid, however he may try to conceal it.

"Aren't you coming? What's the matter?"

Until we're settled in our compartment, or, rather, until

the train has left, my wife is never sure that we're really going to get our vacation.

"What are you bothering about? You're not on duty!"

There have been times when I've followed her with a sigh, turning around for a last look at some mysterious face vanishing in the crowd. Always reluctantly.

And I do not think it is only from professional conscientiousness, or from love of justice.

I repeat, it is a game that's being played, a game that has no end. Once you've begun it, it is difficult, if not impossible, to give it up.

The proof is that those of us who eventually retire, often against their will, almost always set up a private detective agency.

Moreover, that's only a last resort. I do not know one who, after grumbling for thirty years about the miseries of a policeman's life, isn't ready to take up the work again, even without pay.

I have grim memories of the Gare du Nord. I don't know why, but I always picture it full of thick, damp early-morning fog, with drowsy crowds flocking toward the tracks or toward Rue de Maubeuge.

The specimens of humanity I met there were some of the most desperate, and certain arrests I made there left me with a feeling of remorse, rather than of any professional satisfaction.

If, nonetheless, I had the choice, I would rather go on duty again tomorrow at the entrance to the tracks than set off from some more sumptuous station for a sunny corner of the Côte d'Azur.

Stairs, stairs, still more stairs!

From time to time, almost always on the occasion of some political upheaval, troubles break out in the streets that are no longer merely the manifestation of popular discontent. It would seem that at a certain moment a breach is made, invisible sluices are opened, and there suddenly appear in the wealthier districts creatures whose very existence is generally unknown there, who seem to have emerged from some beggars' haunt, and whom the inhabitants watch from their windows as they might watch ruffians and cutthroats suddenly appearing from the depths of the Middle Ages.

What surprised me most, when this phenomenon occurred with notable violence after the riots on February 6, was the astonishment expressed next day by most of the newspapers.

This invasion of the heart of Paris, for a few hours, not by demonstrators, but by haggard individuals who spread as much terror around them as a pack of wolves, suddenly alarmed people who, by their profession, are almost as closely acquainted as we are with the underworld of a capital.

Paris was really frightened that time. Then, the very next day, once order was restored, Paris forgot that this rabble had not been destroyed, that it had simply gone to earth.

Are not the police there to keep order?

Is it generally known that there is one squad solely concerned with the two to three hundred thousand North Africans, Portuguese, and others who live on the outskirts of the Twentieth Arrondissement, who camp out there, one might more accurately say, scarcely knowing our language or not knowing it at all, obeying other laws, other reflexes than our own?

We have, at the Quai des Orfèvres, maps on which are marked little islands, as it were, in colored pencil—the Jews of Rue des Rosiers, the Italians of the Hôtel de Ville district, the Russians of Les Ternes and Denfert-Rochereau . . .

Many of them ask nothing more than to be assimilated, and our difficulties don't come from them, but there are some who, whether as a group or as individuals, stay deliberately on the fringe, and lead their mysterious lives unnoticed by the crowd around them.

Highly respectable people, whose petty frauds and dirty tricks are carefully camouflaged, are almost always the ones who ask me, with that slight quiver of the lips that I know so well:

"Aren't you sometimes disgusted?"

They are not referring to any particular thing, but to the whole group of people we have to deal with. What they would like is to have us disclose really nasty secrets to them, unheard-of vices, a lot of filth at which they could express their horror while secretly relishing it.

Such people often use the phrase "the dregs of society."

"What dreadful things you must see among the dregs of society!"

I prefer not to answer them. I look at them in a certain way, without any expression on my face, and they must understand my meaning, because they generally look uncomfortable and don't ask any more.

I learned a great deal on the public streets. I learned much, too, at fairs and in the big stores, wherever crowds were gathered.

I have spoken of my experiences in the Gare du Nord.

But it was while I covered furnished rooms that I learned most about men, particularly those men who frighten the inhabitants of wealthy districts when the sluices happen to open.

Hobnailed shoes were not needed here, for one's job was not to cover miles of sidewalk but to trudge in a vertical direction, so to speak.

Every day I collected the index cards of some score of the hundreds of hotels, of furnished apartment houses, where there was seldom an elevator, and one had to climb six or seven floors up a stifling staircase, where there was a sickeningly acrid smell of poverty-stricken humanity.

Big hotels with revolving doors flanked by uniformed doormen have their dramas, too, their secrets into which the police pry daily.

But it is chiefly in the thousands of hotels with unfamiliar names, inconspicuous from outside, that a certain floating population goes to earth, a population that is difficult to get hold of elsewhere and seldom law-abiding. We went in pairs. Sometimes, in dangerous districts, we went in larger groups. We would choose the time at which most people were in bed, shortly after midnight.

Then a sort of nightmare would begin, with certain details always recurring, the night watchman, the landlord, or his wife, lying in bed behind the spy hole and waking up unwillingly to try to forestall any accusation.

"You know very well we've never had any trouble here. . . ."

In the old days, the names used to be written in registers. Later, when identity cards became compulsory, there were forms to be filled in.

One of us would stay below. The other went upstairs. Sometimes we were spotted in spite of all our precautions, and from the ground floor we would hear the house beginning to stir like a beehive, busy comings and goings in the rooms, furtive footsteps on the stairs.

Occasionally we would find a room empty, the bed still warm, and at the top of the house the skylight that gave access to the roof would be open.

Usually we managed to reach the first floor without rousing the lodgers, and we would knock at the first door and be answered by grunts, by questions almost invariably in a foreign language.

"Police!"

That's a word they all understand. And then, in their underclothes or stark naked, men, women, and children would scurry about in the dim light, in the stench, unfastening unbelievable trunks to hunt for a passport hidden under their belongings.

There's no describing the anxious look in those eyes, those sleepwalker's movements, and that particular brand of humility that is found only in the uprooted. A proud humility, shall I call it?

They did not hate us. We were the masters. We had—

or they believed we had—the most terrible of all powers: that of sending them back across the frontier.

For some of them the fact of being here represented years of scheming or waiting. They had reached the promised land. They owned papers, real or forged.

And while they held them out to us, afraid that we would thrust them in our pockets, they tried instinctively to win us with a smile, and found a few words of French to stammer:

"Please, Mister Officer . . ."

The women rarely bothered about modesty, and sometimes you would see a hesitant look in their eyes, and they would make a vague gesture toward the tumbled bed. Weren't we tempted? Wouldn't we like to?

And yet all these people had their pride, a special pride that I cannot describe. The pride of wild animals?

Indeed, it was rather like caged beasts that they watched us pass, without knowing whether we were going to strike them or stroke them.

Sometimes we'd see one of them brandishing his papers, panic-stricken, and he'd start talking volubly in his own language, gesticulating, calling the rest to his aid, striving to make us believe that he was an honest man, that appearances were misleading, that . . .

Some would start weeping, and others crouched sullenly in their corner as if they were about to spring, though they were actually resigned.

Identity verification. That's what the operation is called in administrative language. Those whose papers are indisputably in order are allowed to stay in their rooms, where you hear them lock the door with a sigh of relief.

The others . . .

"Come downstairs!"

When they don't understand, you have to add a gesture. And they get dressed, talking to themselves. They don't know what they ought to take or are allowed to take with them. Occasionally, as soon as our backs are turned, they return to get some hidden treasure and thrust it into a pocket or under their shirts.

They all stand there on the ground floor in a small silent group, each thinking only of his own situation and how he is going to defend himself.

In the Saint-Antoine district there are certain hotels where I have found up to seven or eight Poles in a single room, most of them sleeping on the floor.

Only one was inscribed on the register. Did the landlord know? Did he exact payment for the additional sleepers? It's more than likely, but it's useless to try to prove such things.

The others' papers, needless to say, were not in order. What did they do when they had to leave the shelter of the room at daybreak?

For lack of work permits, they could not earn a regular living. But they had not died of starvation. So they must have been eating somehow.

And there were, and still are, thousands, tens of thousands in the same situation.

You may find money in their pockets, or hidden on top of a wardrobe, or, more frequently, in their shoes. Then you have to discover how they procured it, and that's the most exhausting kind of cross-examination.

Even if they understand French, they pretend not to, looking you in the eyes with an expression of good will and tirelessly reasserting their innocence.

It's useless to ask the others about them. They never betray one another. They will all tell the same story.

Now, on an average, sixty-five percent of the crimes committed in the Paris area are due to foreigners.

Stairs, stairs, and still more stairs. Not only at night but by day, and tarts everywhere, professionals and others, some of them young and fine-looking, come, God knows why, from the depths of their own countries.

I knew one of these, a Polish woman, who shared a hotel room on Rue Saint-Antoine with five men, whom she used to send out on robberies, rewarding those who were successful in her own fashion, while the others fretted impatiently in the same room and afterward usually fell savagely upon the exhausted winner.

Two of them were enormous powerful brutes, and she was not afraid of them; she kept them in awe of her with a smile or a frown. While I was questioning them once, in my own office, after some remark or other made in their own language I saw her calmly slap one of these giants in the face.

"You must see all kinds of things!"

Well, we see men and women, all sorts of men and women, in the most unbelievable situations, at every social level. We see them, we take note, and we try to understand.

I do not mean understand some deep human mystery or other. That romantic idea is possibly the thing against which I protest most earnestly, almost angrily. It is one of the reasons for this book, for these attempted corrections.

Simenon has endeavored to explain this, I admit. Nevertheless, I have felt a certain embarrassment on seeing attributed to me in his books certain smiles, certain attitudes I have never assumed, which would have made my colleagues shrug their shoulders.

The person who has understood best is my wife. And yet, when I get back from work, she never questions me with any curiosity, whatever the case I'm concerned with.

For my part, I do not take her into my confidence.

I sit down at the table like any other civil servant who has just come home from work. In a few words, as though for my own benefit, I may describe an encounter, an interview, or talk of the man or woman about whom I am making investigations.

If she asks a question, it is almost always a technical one.

"In which district?"

Or else:

"How old?"

Or again:

"How long has she been in France?"

Because she has come to consider such details to be as revealing as we have ourselves.

She does not question me about sordid or pathetic side issues.

And Heaven knows it's not for lack of feeling!

"Has his wife been to see him at the police station?"

"This morning."

"Did she bring the child with her?"

She takes a particular interest, for reasons on which I need not enlarge, in those who have children, and it would be a mistake to think that lawbreakers, malefactors, and criminals have none.

We had one of these in our own home, a little girl whose mother I had sent to prison for life, but we knew that the father would take her back as soon as he was restored to normal life.

She still comes to see us. She is grown up now, and my wife takes pride in going around the shops with her in the afternoon.

What I want to stress is that our behavior toward those

with whom we have to deal involved neither sentimentality nor hardness, neither hatred nor pity in the usual sense of the word.

Our job is to study men. We watch their behavior. We register facts. We try to establish others.

Our knowledge is in some ways technical.

When, as a young man, I visited a disreputable rooming house from cellar to attic, exploring rooms like cells in a honeycomb, surprising people in their sleep, in their most elementary privacy, examining their papers with a magnifying glass, I could almost foretell what would become of each of them.

For one thing, certain faces were already familiar to me, since Paris is not so big that one doesn't constantly come across the same individuals, in a given area.

Certain cases, too, recur almost identically, the same causes producing the same results.

The wretched Central European who saved for months, if not years, to buy himself a false passport from a clandestine agency in his own country, and who thought his troubles were over once he had safely crossed the border, will inevitably fall into our hands before six months, or twelve at most, have passed.

Indeed, we could even follow him in our mind's eye from the border, and foretell in what district, in what restaurant, in what rooming house he would end up.

We know through whom he will try to procure the indispensable work permit, genuine or forged; then we merely have to go and pick him up in the line that stretches out every morning in front of the big factories of Javel.

Why should we feel anger or resentment when he ends up where he was bound to end up?

The same thing happens with the fresh-faced girl we

see paying her first visit to a certain dance hall. Can we tell her to go back to her employers and keep away from that flashy companion of hers?

It would do no good. She'll come back. We'll meet her at other dance halls, then, one fine evening, outside the door of some hotel in the Halles or Bastille district.

Ten thousand go that way, on an average, every year, ten thousand who leave their villages and start off in domestic service in Paris, and who, before a few months or a few weeks are out, will have taken the plunge.

Is it so very different when a boy of eighteen or twenty, who has been working in a factory, begins to dress in a certain way, to adopt certain poses, to lean on the zinc counters of certain bars?

We will see him soon in a new suit, wearing artificial silk socks and tie.

He'll end up in our hands, too, looking shifty or crest-fallen, after an attempted burglary or robbery, unless he has joined the car thieves' legion.

There are certain signs you cannot mistake, and it was really these signs that we were learning to recognize when we were sent to serve in every squad in turn, to cover miles of sidewalk on foot, climb up stair after stair, and make our way into every sort of slum and among every type of crowd.

That was why the nickname "hobnailed socks" never annoyed us; quite the reverse.

There are few of us at the Quai des Orfèvres who, by the time we are forty, are not well acquainted, for instance, with all the pickpockets. We even know where to find them on such and such a day, on the occasion of such and such a ceremony or festivity.

In the same way, we know, very probably, that there will shortly be a jewel robbery, because a certain specialist who has seldom been caught red-handed has begun to run short of cash. He has left his hotel on Boulevard Haussmann for a more modest one in the République district. He has not paid his bill for two weeks. The woman with whom he's living has begun to have fights with him, and has bought no new hats for a long time.

We cannot follow his step by step; there would never be enough inspectors to shadow every suspect. But we have him on the end of a string. The Public Roads Squad has been warned to keep an eye especially on jewelers' shops. We know his way of working. We know he'll never work any other way.

It isn't always successful. That would be too much to hope for. But it sometimes happens that he's caught in the act. It sometimes happens after a discreet interview with his girl friend, who's been given the hint that her own future would be less problematic if she provided us with information.

The papers talk a great deal about gangs settling accounts with one another in Montmartre or the area around Rue Fontaine, because there's always something exciting for the public about gunshots in the night.

But those are just the affairs that worry us least at the Quai.

We know the rival gangs, their interests and the points at issue between them. We also know their personal hatreds and resentments.

One crime calls forth another, in retaliation. If someone shoots down Luciano in a bar on Rue de Douai, the Corsicans will inevitably take their revenge before very long. And almost always there's one among them who will give us a hint.

"Something's being hatched against Flatfooted Dédé.

He knows it and he won't go out without a couple of killers as bodyguards."

The day Dédé gets his, it's ninety percent certain that a more or less mysterious telephone call will put us in the picture about every detail of the story.

"There's one less!"

We arrest the guilty men, but it really makes little difference, because those people exterminate only one another, for reasons of their own, according to a certain code, which they apply strictly.

It was to this that Simenon was alluding when, during out first interview, he declared so categorically:

"I'm not interested in professionals."

What he did not know then, but has learned since, is that there are very few other sorts of crime.

I am not including crimes of passion, which are straightforward for the most part, being merely the logical issue of an acute crisis between two or more individuals.

I am not including those brawls where a couple of drunks knife one another one Saturday or Sunday night in the slums.

Apart from such accidents, the most frequent crimes are of two sorts:

The murder of some lonely old woman by one or more hoodlums, and the killing of a prostitute in some empty lot.

In the first case, the culprit rarely escapes. Almost always he is one of those youngsters I mentioned before, who quit factory work a few months back, and is dying to show off his toughness.

He has had his eye on some tobacconist's or haberdasher's, some small shop in a quiet back street.

Sometimes he's bought a revolver. Other times he makes do with a hammer or wrench.

Almost invariably he knows his victim, and, in at least one case out of ten, she has done him a kindness at some time or another.

He has not planned to kill. He has put a scarf over his face so as not to be recognized.

The scarf slips, or else the old woman begins to scream.

He fires. He strikes. If he fires, he empties the whole cylinder, which is a sign of panic. If he strikes, he strikes ten or twenty blows, savagely, it seems, but really because he's out of his mind with terror.

It will not surprise you that, when we have him in front of us, in a state of collapse and yet still trying to swagger, we merely say to him:

"You fool!"

They almost always pay with their lives. The least they can get away with is twenty years, when they're lucky enough to interest some first-rate counsel.

As for the murderers of prostitutes, it is only by a miracle that we lay hands on them. These investigations are the longest, the most discouraging, the most sickening I know.

They usually begin with a sack being fished up by some waterman on the end of his boat hook, somewhere along the Seine, and containing, almost always, a mutilated body. The head is missing, or an arm, or both legs.

Weeks go by before identification is possible. Generally, the victim is one of those elderly whores who don't even take their customers to a hotel or to their room, but make do with some doorway or the shelter of a fence.

She hasn't been seen lately in her neighborhood, one of those districts that, as soon as night falls, becomes full of mystery and silent shadows.

The women who knew her are not anxious to get in

touch with us. When we question them, they give only the vaguest answers.

Eventually, by dint of patience, we manage, after a fashion, to discover some of her usual clients, lonely individuals themselves, solitary men of indefinite age who are remembered merely as shadowy figures.

Was she killed for her money? It is hardly likely. She had so little!

Had one of these old fellows suddenly gone crazy, or did someone come from elsewhere, from another district, one of those maniacs who, at regular intervals, feeling a fit coming on, know exactly what they will do and, with incredible lucidity, take precautions of which other criminals are incapable?

No one knows how many there are of these. There are some in every capital city, who, when the deed is done, disappear once more, for a greater or lesser length of time, into anonymity.

They may be respectable people, fathers of families, model employees.

Nobody knows exactly what they are like, and when by chance we catch one of them, it has almost always been impossible to establish a satisfactory opinion.

We possess more or less exact statistics for crimes of every sort.

Except one.

Poisoning.

And any rough guess would inevitably err in one direction or the other.

Every three months, or six months, in Paris or in the provinces, particularly in the provinces, in some very small town or in the country, a doctor happens by chance to examine a dead body more closely than usual and is puzzled by certain symptoms.

I say chance, for the dead man is usually one of his patients, somebody he has known to be ill for a long time. The man has died suddenly, in his bed, in the bosom of his family, who display all the traditional signs of grief.

The relatives dislike the suggestion of an autopsy. The doctor insists on one only if his suspicions are strong enough.

Or else, weeks after the funeral, an anonymous letter reaches the police, providing details that at first sight seem incredible.

I stress this to show all the conditions that must be combined before an investigation can be opened. The administrative formalities are complicated.

The commonest case is that of a farmer's wife who has been waiting for years for her husband to die in order to set up house with the farm hand, and who has lost patience.

She has helped Nature, as some people crudely put it.

Sometimes, though more rarely, a man will use the same method to get rid of an ailing wife who has become a dead weight in his home.

They are found out by chance. But how many other cases are there where chance does not play its part? We don't know. We can only risk hypotheses. There are some of us at the Quai, as there are in the Rue des Saussaies, who believe that of all crimes, particularly of those that go unpunished, this particular kind is the most frequent.

The others, those that interest novelists and so-called psychologists, are so unusual that they are only an insignificant part of our activities.

But that is the part with which the public is most familiar. These are the cases about which Simenon has written most and will, I suppose, go on writing.

I refer to those crimes that are committed suddenly in the most unlikely settings, which are the final outcome of something that has been brewing for a long time in secret.

A well-kept, prosperous street in Paris or elsewhere. People who have a comfortable house, a family life, an honorable profession.

We have never had occasion to cross their threshold. Often the milieu is one to which we would normally not have access, where our presence would jar, where we would feel awkward, to say the least.

Now somebody has died a violent death, and so we come and ring at the door, and find ourselves confronted by inscrutable faces, by a family of which each member seems to have his own secret.

Here the experience acquired through years on the street, in stations, in rooming houses is no longer useful. Nor is that sort of instinctive respect felt by small fry for authority, for the police.

Nobody here is afraid of being sent back over the border. Nobody is going to be taken off to an office at the Quai to be subjected for hours to a painstaking interrogation, gone over again and again.

The people we have before us are those highly respectable ones who in other circumstances would have asked us:

"Don't you sometimes feel disgusted?"

We do, in these very homes. Not immediately. Not invariably. Because the job is long and chancy.

Even when a telephone call from some minister, some deputy, some important public figure does not try to divert us from our path.

There is a whole varnish of respectability to be cracked off little by little; there are family secrets, more or less repulsive, which they all combine to conceal from us and which have to be brought to light, regardless of protests and threats.

Sometimes five or six of them, or more, may have conspired to lie on certain points, while surreptitiously endeavoring to get the rest into trouble.

Simenon is apt to describe me as awkward and grumbling, feeling ill at ease, glancing at people furtively and with a cantankerous way of barking out my questions.

It is in such cases as these that he has seen me thus, faced with what one might call "amateur" crimes, which one *invariably* discovers, in the end, to have been committed from motives of self-interest.

Not for money. I don't mean crimes committed because of an urgent need for money, as in the case of those petty hoodlums who murder old women.

The interests involved, behind these façades, are more complicated; they are long-term interests, coupled with a concern for respectability. Often the matter goes back many years, concealing a whole lifetime of intrigue and dishonesty.

When these people, brought to bay, finally confess, the whole revolting story comes out, almost always with a panic fear of consequences.

"Surely it's impossible for our family to be dragged in the mud? There must be some way out."

That does happen, I'm sorry to say. Some people who should have left my office only for a cell at the Santé prison have disappeared from circulation, because there are certain influences against which a police inspector, even a chief inspector, is powerless.

"Don't you sometimes feel disgusted?"

I never did when I spent my days or my nights climbing

the stairs of squalid, overcrowded rooming houses, where every door disclosed some distressing or dramatic scene.

Nor does the word "disgust" convey my reaction to the thousands of professionals of every sort who have passed through my hands.

They have played their game and lost. Almost all of them prided themselves on being good losers, and some of them, after they had been sentenced, asked me to visit them in prison, where we chatted like old friends.

I could mention several who begged me to be present at their execution and saved their last dying look for me.

"I'll be all right, you'll see!"

They did their best. They were not always successful. I used to take away in my pocket their last letters, which I had promised to send, with a covering note of my own.

When I got home, my wife had only to look at me, without asking questions, to know how things had gone.

As for the other cases, on which I prefer not to dwell, she was well acquainted with the meaning of certain angry moods of mine, a certain way of sitting down when I got home at night, and of filling my plate, and she never pressed me.

Which is ample proof that she was not destined for Bridges and Highways!

7

*Of a morning as triumphant as a cavalry trumpet
and a young fellow who was no longer thin,
but who had not yet grown really stout*

I can still recall the taste and the color of the sunlight that morning. It was in March. Spring had come early. I had already made it a habit to go on foot, whenever I could, from Boulevard Richard-Lenoir to Quai des Orfèvres.

I had no outside work that day, only files to sort for my section, in what were probably the gloomiest offices in the whole Palais de Justice, on the ground floor, with a little door leading into the courtyard, which I had left open.

I kept as close to it as my work allowed. I remember the sun cutting the courtyard exactly in two, and also cutting across a waiting police wagon. From time to time its two horses stamped on the paving stones, and behind them there was a fine heap of gleaming dung, smoking in the keen morning air.

I don't know why the courtyard reminded me of recess at school, at the same season of the year, when the air suddenly begins to have a special fragrance and, when you've been running, your skin smells of spring.

I was alone in the office. The telephone rang.

"Will you tell Maigret the Chief wants him?"

The voice of the old office clerk upstairs, who had been in his job nearly fifty years.

"It's Maigret."

"Come up then."

Even the great staircase, which was always full of dust, seemed gay, with rays of sunlight slanting down, the way they do in churches. The morning conference had just ended. Two inspectors still stood talking, with their files under their arms, by the Chief's door, which I went up to and knocked on.

And inside the office I could still smell the pipes and cigarettes of those who had just gone out. A window was open behind Xavier Guichard, who had plumes of sunlight in his silky white hair.

He did not hold out his hand to me. He seldom did so in the office. And yet we had become friends, or, more precisely, he had been good enough to honor my wife and me with his friendship. On one occasion, the first, he had invited me alone to his apartment on Boulevard Saint-Germain. Not the wealthy, fashionable part of the boulevard. He lived, on the contrary, right opposite Place Maubert, in a big new building that rose amid rickety houses and squalid hotels.

I had gone back there with my wife. They had immediately got on very well together.

He was undoubtedly fond of her, and of me, and yet he had often hurt us without meaning to.

In the beginning, as soon as he saw Louise, he would start insistently at her figure and, if we seemed not to understand, he would say, with a little cough:

111

"Don't forget that I want to be godfather."

He was a confirmed bachelor. Apart from his brother, who was chief of the municipal police, he had no relatives in Paris.

"Come now, don't keep me waiting too long. . . ."

The years had passed. He must have misunderstood. I remember that when he told me about my first raise, he had added:

"Perhaps that will enable you to give me a godson."

He never understood why we blushed, why my wife lowered her eyes, while I tried to touch her hand to comfort her.

He was looking very serious that morning, seen against the light. He left me standing, and I felt embarrassed by the serious way in which he examined me from head to foot, the way a sergeant looks over a recruit.

"Do you know, Maigret, you're putting on weight?"

I was thirty. Little by little I had stopped being thin, my shoulders had broadened, my chest had expanded, but I had not yet become really stout.

I was conscious of it. I must have seemed flabby in those days, with a somewhat babyish look. It struck me when I passed by a shop window and cast an anxious glance at my silhouette.

It was too much or too little, and no clothes fit me.

"I think I'm getting fatter, yes."

I almost wanted to apologize and I had not yet realized that he was joking, as he loved to do:

"I think I'd better transfer you to another section."

There were two squads in which I had not yet served, the Sports Squad and the Financial Squad, and the latter was my nightmare, just as the trigonometry exam had long been the terror of the end of the school year.

"How old are you?"

"Thirty."

"The right age! That's fine. Young Lesueur will take your place in the Hotels Squad from now on, and you will put yourself at Inspector Guillaume's disposal."

He deliberately said this in an unemphatic tone, as if it were something quite trivial, knowing that my heart was going to leap in my breast and that, as I stood before him there, I could hear triumphant clarion calls ringing in my ears.

Suddenly, on a morning that seemed to have been chosen on purpose—and I'm not sure that Guichard hadn't done so—the dream of my life was being realized.

At last I was to enter the Special Squad.

A quarter of an hour later, I moved upstairs with my old office jacket, my soap and towel, my pencils and some papers.

There were five or six men in the big room reserved for inspectors of the Homicide, or Crime, Squad, and before calling me, Inspector Guillaume let me settle in, like a new pupil.

"A drink on it?"

I wasn't going to say no. At noon I proudly took my new colleagues to the Brasserie Dauphine.

I had often seen them there, at a different table from the one I shared with my former comrades, and we used to watch them with the envious respect felt by schoolboys for older students who are as tall as their teachers and are treated almost on an equal footing.

The comparison was an apt one, for Guillaume was with us, and the superintendent of General Information came to join us.

"What'll you have?" I asked.

In my old corner, we used to drink half-pints of beer, seldom an apéritif. Obviously that wouldn't do for this table.

Somebody said:

"A mandarin-curaçao."

"Mandarins all round?"

Since nobody objected, I ordered I don't know how many mandarins. It was the first time I had tasted one. In the intoxication of my triumph, it seemed to me barely alcoholic.

"Another round?"

Wasn't this the moment, if ever, to show myself generous? We had three each; we had four. My new chief insisted on paying for a round, too.

The city was full of sunlight. The streets were steaming with it. The women in their bright dresses were a delight. I threaded my way between pedestrians. I looked at myself in shop windows and thought I wasn't so fat after all.

I ran. I flew. I exulted. As soon as I reached the foot of the stairs, I began, ahead of time, the speech I had prepared for my wife.

And going up the last flight, I fell flat. I hadn't had time to get up again when our door opened, for Louise must have been getting anxious at my delay.

"Have you hurt yourself?"

It was funny. At the precise moment when I stood up again, I felt completely drunk, and was amazed at it. The staircase was whirling around me. My wife's figure was blurred. She seemed to have at least two mouths and three or four eyes.

Believe it or not, it was the first time in my life that this had happened to me, and I felt so humiliated that I dared not look at her. I slunk into the apartment like a guilty one without remembering the triumphant phrases I had so carefully prepared.

"I think . . . I think I'm a little drunk."

I was painfully sniffling. The table was laid, with our two places opposite one another in front of the open window. I had promised myself to take her out to lunch at a restaurant, but I dared not propose it now.

So it was in an almost gloomy tone that I announced:

"It's happened!"

"What's happened?"

Perhaps she was expecting me to tell her that I'd been shown the door by the police.

"I've been appointed."

"Appointed what?"

Apparently I had great tears in my eyes, tears of vexation but also, no doubt, of joy, as I let fall the words:

"To the Special Squad."

"Sit down. I'm going to make you a cup of strong black coffee."

She tried to get me to lie down, but I was not going to desert my new post on the first day. I drank I don't know how many cups of strong coffee. In spite of Louise's insistence, I couldn't swallow any solid food. I took a shower.

At two o'clock, when I went to the Quai des Orfèvres, my cheeks had a peculiar rosy glow, my eyes were glittering. I felt limp and light-headed.

I went to sit in my corner and spoke as little as possible, because I knew that my voice was unsteady and that I might get my syllables mixed up.

Next day, as though to put me to the test, they entrusted me with my first arrest. It was on Rue du Roi-de-Sicile, in a rooming house. The man had been shadowed for five days already. He was responsible for several murders. He was a foreigner, a Czech, if I remember rightly, a strong fellow, invariably armed, invariably on the alert.

The problem was to immobilize him before he had time to defend himself, because he was the sort of man who would fire into a crowd, kill as many people as possible, before letting himself be brought down.

He knew that he was at the end of his tether, that the police were on his heels but were still hesitating.

Out of doors he always managed to stay in the middle of a crowd, well aware that we could take no risks.

I was sent as assistant to Inspector Dufour, who had been following the man for several days and knew all his movements.

This was the first time, too, that I disguised myself. To have appeared in that sordid hotel dressed as we usually were would have provoked a panic, under cover of which our man might have escaped.

Dufour and I put on old clothes and, to make things more convincing, went forty-eight hours without shaving.

A young inspector, a skilled locksmith, had got into the hotel and had then made us an excellent key to the man's room.

We took a room on the same floor, before the Czech came back to bed. It was just after eleven when a signal from outside warned us that he was coming up the stairs.

The tactics we followed were not suggested by me, but by Dufour, an old hand at the game.

The man, not far away from us, had shut his door and was lying fully clothed on his bed, and he probably had at least a loaded revolver within reach.

We did not sleep. We waited for dawn. If you ask me why, I will give the answer my colleague, to whom I put the same question, gave me.

The murderer's first reflex, on hearing us, would undoubtedly have been to smash the gas burner in his room. We would thus have been in darkness, and he would have had an advantage over us.

"A man's resistance is always lower in the early morning," Dufour told me, and I've confirmed this subsequently.

We crept into the hallway. Everybody was asleep around us. Taking infinite care, Dufour turned the key in the lock.

Since I was the tallest and the heaviest, it was my job to rush forward first, and I did so, in one bound, and found myself on top of the man as he lay stretched out on the bed, grabbing him by whatever I could get hold of.

I don't know how long the struggle went on, but it seemed to me interminable. I felt myself rolling on the floor with him. I could see a fierce face close to my own. I remember particularly a set of huge dazzling teeth. A hand, clutching my ear, was trying to wrench it off.

I was not conscious of what my colleague was doing, but I saw an expression of pain and rage on my opponent's face. I felt him gradually loosen his hold. When I was able to turn around, Inspector Dufour, sitting cross-legged on the floor, was holding one of the man's feet in his hand, and it looked as if he'd been giving it at least a double twist.

"Handcuffs," he ordered.

I had already handcuffed less dangerous prisoners, such as refractory prostitutes. This was the first time I had carried out a forcible arrest, and the sound of handcuffs put an end for me to a fight that might have ended badly.

When people talk about a policeman's flair, or his methods, his intuition, I always want to answer:

"What about your shoemaker's flair, or your baker's?"

Both of these have gone through years of apprenticeship. Each of them knows his job and everything concerned with it.

The same is true of a man from the Quai des Orfèvres. And that is why all the stories I have read, including those of my friend Simenon, are more or less inaccurate.

We sit in our office, writing reports. For this is also part of the job, a fact too frequently forgotten. I might even say that we spend far more time over administrative red tape than on actual investigations.

We are told that a middle-aged gentleman is in the waiting room, looking very nervous and asking to speak to the chief immediately. Needless to say, the chief doesn't have time to receive all the people who turn up and want a personal interview because their little problem, to them, is the only important one.

There is one phrase that recurs so often that it has become like a refrain, and the receptionist recites it like a litany: "A matter of life and death?"

"Are you seeing him, Maigret?"

There is a little room next to the inspectors' office for such interviews as these.

"Sit down. Cigarette?"

More often than not, before the visitor had had time to tell us his profession and his social status we have guessed them.

"It's a very delicate matter, quite personal."

A bank teller, or an insurance agent, a man with a quiet, regular way of life.

"Your daughter?"

It's either his son or his daughter or his wife. And we can guess almost word for word the speech he's going to pour forth to us. No. His son hasn't taken money out of the boss's cashbox. Nor has his wife gone off with a young man.

It's his daughter, a very well-brought-up young girl, about whom there has never been a word of criticism. She saw nobody, lived at home, and helped her mother with the housework.

Her girl friends were as serious-minded as she was. She practically never went out alone.

And yet she's vanished, taking some of her belongings with her.

What can you tell him? That six hundred people disappear every month in Paris and that about two-thirds of them are found?

"Is your daughter very pretty?"

He has brought several photographs, convinced that they'll be useful in our search. If she's pretty, so much the worse, for the number of chances is lessened. If she's ugly, on the contrary, she'll probably come back in a few days, or a few weeks.

"You can rely on us. We'll do what's necessary."

"When?"

"Right away."

He's going to call us up every day, twice a day, and there is nothing to tell him, except that we haven't had time to look for the young lady.

Almost always a brief inquiry reveals that a young man living in the same apartment house, or the grocer's assistant, or the brother of one of her girl friends has disappeared on the same day she did.

You cannot go through Paris and France with a fine-tooth comb for a runaway girl, and her photograph will merely go next week to join the collection of prints sent to police stations, to the various branches of the service and to frontier posts.

• • •

Eleven o'clock at night. A telephone call from the police emergency center, across the street, in the building of the municipal police, where all calls are inscribed on an illuminated board that takes up the whole length of a wall.

The Pont-de-Flandre station has just heard that there's been trouble in a bar on Rue de Crimée.

It is right on the other side of Paris. Today, the Police Judiciaire has a few cars at its disposal, but formerly you had to take a carriage, later a taxi, for which you couldn't be sure you'd be reimbursed.

The bar, at a street corner, is still open, with a broken window, figures standing prudently at some distance, because in that district people prefer not to attract the attention of the police.

Uniformed policemen are there already, an ambulance, sometimes the district superintendent or his assistant.

On the ground, in the sawdust and spittle, a man lies crumpled up, one hand on his breast, from which a trickle of blood is flowing to form a pool.

"Dead!"

Beside him on the floor, a small suitcase, which he was holding when he fell, has burst open, spilling out some pornographic postcards.

The anxious barkeeper tries to clear himself.

"Everything was quiet, as usual. This is a respectable place."

"Had you seen him before?"

"Never."

The answer was inevitable. He probably knows him very well, but he'll go on asserting to the end that it was the first time the man had set foot in his bar.

"What happened?"

The dead man is a drab figure, middle-aged, or, rather,

of indeterminate age. His clothes are old, of doubtful cleanliness; his shirt collar is black with grime.

Useless to hunt for relatives or a home. He must have been staying in the cheapest type of furnished lodgings, at a weekly rate, and set off from there to hawk his wares in the neighborhood of the Tuileries and the Palais-Royal.

"There were three or four customers. . . ."

No point in asking where they are. They've flown away, and will not come back to give evidence.

"Did you know them?"

"Vaguely. By sight only."

Of course! We could give his answers for him.

"A stranger came in and sat down at the other side of the bar, just opposite this fellow."

The bar is horseshoe-shaped, and has overturned glasses on it and a strong smell of cheap liquor.

"They didn't speak to each other. This fellow looked frightened. He put his hand into his pocket to pay. . . ."

That is so, because he had no weapon on him.

"The other never said a word, but pulled out his gun and fired three times. He'd have gone on probably if his revolver hadn't jammed. Then he calmly pulled his hat down over his eyes and went out."

That's clear enough. No need to nose out more here. The milieu in which we have to hunt is a particularly restricted one.

There aren't so many of them who peddle dirty pictures. We know exactly all of them. Periodically they pass through our hands, serve a short sentence in jail, and then begin again.

The dead man's shoes—his feet are dirty, and there are holes in his socks—bear the name of a Berlin firm.

He is a newcomer. He must have been given a hint that there was no room for him in the district. Or else he was a subordinate to whom the goods were entrusted and who had kept the money for himself.

It will take three days, four perhaps. Hardly longer. The Hotels Squad will promptly be called upon to help and, before the next night, will know where the victim was staying.

The Morals Squad, armed with his photograph, will pursue their separate inquiry.

That afternoon, in the neighborhood of the Tuileries, they'll arrest some of those individuals who all offer passers-by the same trash with an air of mystery.

They won't be very nice to them. In the old days, they were even less so than they are today.

"Have you ever seen this fellow?"

"No."

"Are you sure you've never met him?"

There's a certain little cell, very dark, very narrow, a sort of closet really, on the mezzanine floor, where people like that are helped to remember, and it seldom happens that after a few hours they don't start banging on the door.

"I think I've caught sight of him. . . ."

"His name?"

"I only know his first name: Otto."

The skein will unwind slowly, but it will unwind to the end, like a tapeworm.

"He's queer!"

Good! The fact that a homosexual is involved restricts the field of inquiry still further.

"Didn't he often go to Rue de Bondy?"

It was almost inevitable. There's a certain little bar there frequented by practically all homosexuals of a certain social level—the lowest. There's another on Rue de Lappe, which has become an attraction for tourists.

"Who have you seen him with?"

That's about all. It only remains, when we get the man within four walls, to make him confess and sign his confession.

All cases are not as simple as that. Some investigations take months. And certain criminals are eventually arrested only after long years, and then sometimes by pure chance.

In practically every case, the process is the same.

You have to *know*.

To know the milieu in which a crime has been committed, to know the way of life, the habits, morals, reactions of the people involved in it, whether victims, criminals, or merely witnesses.

To enter into their world without surprise, easily, and to speak its language naturally.

This is as true whether we are concerned with a bistro in La Villette or with one near the Porte d'Italie, with Arabs in the Zone or with Poles or Italians, with the street-walkers of Pigalle or the young delinquents of Les Ternes.

It's still true whether we are concerned with the racing world or the gambling world, with safe-breaking specialists or jewel thieves.

That is why we are not wasting our time when we spend years pacing the sidewalks, climbing stairs, or lying in wait for shoplifters in big stores.

Like the shoemaker, like the baker, we are serving our apprenticeship, with this difference: that it goes on for practically the whole of our lives, because the number of milieus is almost infinite.

Prostitutes, pickpockets, cardsharps, confidence men, or specialists in check forgery recognize one another.

One might say the same of policemen after a certain number of years on the job. And it's not a matter of hobnailed shoes or mustaches.

I think it's the look in our eyes that gives us away, a certain reaction—or, rather, lack of reaction—when confronted with certain creatures, certain states of destitution, certain anomalies.

With all due deference to novelists, a policeman is, above all, a professional. He is an *official*.

He's not engaged in a guessing game, or in getting excited over a more or less thrilling chase.

When he spends a night in the rain, watching a door that doesn't open or a lighted window, when he patiently scans the sidewalk cafés on the boulevards for a familiar face, or prepares to spend hours questioning a pale, terrified individual, he is doing his daily job.

He is earning his living, trying to earn, as honestly as possible, the money that the government gives him at the end of every month in remuneration for his services.

I know that my wife, when she reads these lines presently, will shake her head and look at me reproachfully, murmuring, maybe:

"You always exaggerate!"

She will probably add:

"You're going to give the wrong idea of yourself and your colleagues."

She's quite right. I may possibly be exaggerating somewhat in the contrary direction. It's by way of reaction against the ready-made ideas that have so often irritated me.

How many times, after the publication of one of Simenon's books, have my colleagues looked at me mockingly as I went into my office!

I could read in their eyes what they were thinking: "Well, here comes God the Father!"

That is why I insist on the term "official," which others consider derogatory.

I have been an official almost all my life. Thanks to Inspector Jacquemain, I became one on the threshold of manhood.

Just as my father, in his day, became estate manager at the château. With the same pride. With the same concern to know everything about my job and to carry out my task conscientiously.

The difference between other officials and those of the Quai des Orfèvres is that the latter are, as it were, balanced between two worlds.

By their dress, by their education, by their homes and their way of life, they are indistinguishable from other middle-class people and share their dream of a little house in the country.

Most of their time is spent nonetheless in contact with the underworld, the riffraff, the dregs, often with the enemies of organized society.

This has often struck me. It's a strange situation about which I have sometimes felt uneasy.

I live in a bourgeois apartment, where the savory smells of my carefully prepared dinner await me, where everything is simple and neat, clean and comfortable. Through my windows I see only homes like my own, mothers walking with their children along the boulevard, housewives going to do their shopping.

I belong to that social group, of course, to what are known as respectable people.

But I know the others, too; I know them well enough for a certain contact to exist between myself and them.

The tarts at the brasserie on Place de la République, when I go by, know that I understand their language and the meaning of their attitudes. So does the street Arab threading his way through the crowd.

And all the others whom I have met and still meet every day, under the most intimate conditions.

Isn't this enough to make some sort of bond?

It's not my business to make excuses for them, to justify or absolve them. It's not my business, either, to adorn them with some sort of halo, as was the fashion at one time.

It's my business simply to consider them as a fact, to look at them with the eye of one who knows them.

Without curiosity, because curiosity is quickly dulled.

Without hatred, of course.

To look at them, in short, as creatures who exist and who, for the well-being of society, for the sake of the established order, have got to be kept, willy-nilly, within certain bounds and punished when they overstep them.

They are well aware of this themselves! They bear us no grudge for it. They often say:

"You're doing your job."

As for what they think of that particular job, I'd rather not try to find out.

Is it surprising that after twenty-five or thirty years with the police we walk with a rather heavy step, and have in our eyes an even heavier look, sometimes a blank look?

"Don't you sometimes feel disgusted?"

No, I don't! And it's probably through my job that I have acquired a fairly unshakable optimism.

Paraphrasing a saying of my first catechism teacher, I would like to say: a little knowledge turns one away from man; a great deal of knowledge brings one back to man.

It is because I have witnessed depravities of every sort that I have come to realize that they were compensated by a great deal of simple courage, good will, or resignation.

Utterly rotten individuals are rare, and most of those I have come across, unfortunately, functioned out of my reach, out of our sphere of action.

As for the rest, I tried to prevent them from doing too much harm and to see to it that they paid for the harm they had already done.

After which, surely, we've settled our accounts.

That chapter is closed.

Place des Vosges, a young woman's engagement,
and some little notes from Madame Maigret

"On the whole," Louise said, "I don't see all that much difference."

I always look rather anxiously at her when she's reading what I have just been writing, trying to forestall her criticisms.

"Difference between what?"

"Between what you say about yourself and what Simenon says about you."

"Oh!"

"Perhaps I'm wrong to give my opinion."

"No, no, of course not!"

All the same, if she is right, I've given myself needless trouble. And it's quite possible that she is right, that I haven't known how to go about it, how to set things out as I had promised myself.

Or else the famous tirade about made-up truths being truer than naked truths is not a mere paradox.

I have done my best. Only there are heaps of things that struck me as essential at the beginning, points I had determined to develop and that I have abandoned on the way.

For instance, one shelf of the bookcase is full of Simenon's books, which I have patiently stuffed with blue pencil marks, and I was looking forward to correcting all the mistakes he's made, either because he didn't know, or else for the sake of being picturesque, often because he didn't have the courage to call me up to verify some detail.

What's the use? I would look like a fussy fellow, and I'm beginning to believe myself that these things are not so very important.

One of his habits that irritated me most sometimes was that of mixing up dates, of setting at the beginning of my career investigations that took place much later on, and vice versa, so that sometimes my inspectors are described as being quite young, whereas they were really staid fathers of families at the period in question, or the other way around.

I had even thought seriously—I confess it now that I've given up the idea—of establishing, thanks to the files of newspaper clippings my wife has kept up to date, a chronology of the principal cases in which I've been involved.

"Why not?" Simenon replied. "Excellent idea. They'll be able to correct my books for the next edition."

He added, without irony:

"Only, Maigret old fellow, you'll have to be kind enough to do the job yourself, because I've never had the courage to reread my own books."

I have said what I had to say, on the whole, and it cannot be helped if I've said it badly. My colleagues will understand, and everyone who's more or less connected with our work, and it's chiefly for them that I was anxious to get things straight, to speak not so much of myself as of our profession.

It looks as if some important question escaped me. I hear my wife carefully opening the door of the dining room, where I am working, and tiptoeing forward.

She has just put a scrap of paper on the table before withdrawing in the same fashion. I read these penciled words:

"Place des Vosges."

And I can't resist smiling with private satisfaction, since this proves that she, too, has details to get right, one at least, and, actually, for the same reason as mine, out of loyalty.

In her case, it is out of loyalty to our apartment on Boulevard Richard-Lenoir, which we have never deserted, which still belongs to us today, although we use it only a few days a year now that we're living in the country.

In several of his books Simenon described us as living on Place des Vosges, without offering the slightest explanation.

I'm giving my wife's message then. It is quite true that for a number of months we lived on Place des Vosges. But we were not in our own home.

That year our landlord had at last decided to get the building refaced, which it had been needing for some time. In front of the house, workmen set up scaffolding, which covered our windows. Others, inside, began making holes in the walls and floor to install central heating. We had been promised that it would take three weeks at most. After two weeks they had got nowhere, and just at that time a strike was declared in the building trades, and nobody knew how long it might last.

Simenon was just off for Africa, where he was to spend nearly a year.

"Why don't you move into my apartment on Place des Vosges until the job's finished?"

And so it happened that we went to live there, at Number 21, to be exact, without incurring the reproach of disloyalty to our dear old boulevard.

There was one period, too, in which, without warning me, he made me retire, when I still had several years' service to go.

We had just bought our house at Meung-sur-Loire and we used to spend all my free Sundays getting it ready. He came to visit us there. The place delighted him so much that in the next book he quite shamelessly anticipated events, made me several years older, and settled me there for good.

"It makes a change of atmosphere," he told me when I spoke to him about it. *"I was getting bored with the Quai des Orfèvres."*

Allow me to underline that sentence, which seems to me outrageous. It is he, you notice, who was getting bored with the Quai, with my office, with the daily work of the Police Judiciaire!

Which did not prevent him subsequently, and will probably not prevent him in future, from relating earlier investigations, still giving no dates, making me sometimes sixty years old and sometimes forty-five.

Here's my wife again. I have no study at home. I don't need one. When I have to work, I settle down at the dining-room table, and Louise retires into the kitchen, which does not displease her. I look at her, thinking she wants to tell me something. But it's another scrap of paper she has in her hand and she has come to lay it timidly in front of me.

This time it is a list, as when I'm going out and she writes down on a scrap torn out of her notebook what I have to bring back to her.

My nephew heads the list, and I understand why. He's her sister's son. I got him into the police a long time ago, at an age when he was fired with enthusiasm for it.

Simenon mentioned him, then the boy suddenly disappeared from his books, and I can guess Louise's scruples. She's been thinking that for some readers this may have appeared suspicious, as though her nephew had committed some stupidity.

The truth is quite simple. He had not done as brilliantly as he had hoped. And he did not put up much resistance to his father-in-law's pressing offers of a place in his soap factory in Marseilles.

The name Torrence comes next on the list, big noisy Torrence (I believe that somewhere or other Simenon makes him die in place of another inspector who was in fact killed by my side in a Champs-Elysées hotel).

Torrence had no father-in-law in soap. But he had a terrific appetite for life, together with a business sense that was hardly compatible with the existence of an official.

He left us to establish a private detective agency, a highly respectable agency, I hasten to add, for that is not always the case. And for a long time he kept on coming to the Quai to ask for our help, or for information, or merely to breathe the atmosphere of the place again.

He has a big American car, which stops from time to time in front of our door, and each time he is accompanied by a pretty woman, always a different one, whom he introduces with unvarying sincerity as his fiancée.

I read the third name, Little Janvier, as we have always called him. He is still at the Quai. Probably they still call him Little Janvier?

In his last letter he informed me, not without a certain melancholy, that his daughter is engaged to a young man from the Ecole Polytechnique.

Finally, Lucas, who, at the present moment, is probably sitting as usual in my office, at my desk, smoking one of my pipes, which he begged me, with tears in his eyes, to leave him as a memento.

There's one word at the bottom of the list. I thought at first it was a name, but I couldn't decipher it.

I have just gone into the kitchen, where I was quite surprised to see bright sunlight, since I had closed the shutters in order to work in a half-light I find helpful.

"Finished?"

"No. There's one word I can't read."

She was quite embarrassed.

"It doesn't matter at all."

"What is it?"

"Nothing. Don't pay any attention to it."

Of course I insisted.

"Sloe gin!" she admitted at last, averting her head.

She knew I would burst out laughing, as in fact I did.

When it was a question of my famous bowler hat, my velvet-collared overcoat, my coal stove and my poker, I was well aware that she thought I was being childish when I insisted on making corrections.

Nevertheless, she has herself scribbled the words "sloe gin" at the bottom of the list, making them illegible on purpose, I'm convinced, out of a sort of shame, rather like when she adds to the list of errands to be done some very feminine article she rather shamefacedly asks me to buy for her.

Simenon has mentioned a certain bottle we always had in our sideboard on Boulevard Richard-Lenoir—we still have it there—and of which my sister-in-law, according to a hallowed tradition, brings us a supply from Alsace after her annual visit there.

He has thoughtlessly described it as sloe gin.

Actually, it is raspberry brandy. And for an Alsatian, apparently, this makes a tremendous difference.

"I've made the correction, Louise. Your sister will be satisfied."

This time I left the kitchen door open.

"Nothing else?"

"Tell the Simenons I'm knitting socks for . . ."

"But I'm not writing them a letter, you know!"

"Of course. Make a note of it for when you do write. They're not to forget the photo they promised us."

She added:

"Can I set the table?"

That's all.

Meung-sur-Loire
Sept. 27, 1950